THE TEXAS TATTLER

All the news that's barely fit to print!

"Wrong" Baby Rescued
Will the Real Father Please Stand Up?

A sigh of relief turned into hysteria earlier this week when a child recovered by the FBI and thought to be the abducted Bryan Fortune was actually an unidentified boy of roughly the same age. Blood tests and the distinctive crown-shaped birthmark confirm that the child is, however, a Fortune. Scandalous! Kidnappers remain at large.

The mystery child, "Taylor," is being cared for at the jaw-dropping 500,000-acre Fortune "Western paradise," but no word yet on the identity of the child's father. Looks like one Fortune boy's past just caught up to him— and is wearing a diaper.

Now, is this any time for company at the Double Crown Ranch? Insider sources verify that unwed Savannah Clark, college chum to Vanessa Fortune, arrived on the mansion doorstep yesterday hefting luggage and carrying a secret...in her belly. Better make that room for two more! Is there *another* undisclosed daddy in the house?

About the Author

MARIE FERRARELLA

sold her first contemporary romance to Silhouette
Books fifteen years ago, and has recently been named
to Silhouette's exclusive Five Star Club, having sold
more than five million copies of her books. Her
romances are beloved by fans worldwide and have
been translated into Spanish, Italian, German,
Russian, Polish, Japanese and Korean.

Having earned a master's degree in Shakespearean
comedy, her writing is distinguished by humor and
realistic dialogue. Marie Ferrarella describes herself as
the tired mother of two overenergetic children and
the contented wife of one wonderful man. This RITA
Award-winning author is thrilled to be following her
dream of writing full-time.

Look for these titles by Marie Ferrarella:
HERO IN THE NICK OF TIME
October 1999
Silhouette Intimate Moments

THE BABY BENEATH THE MISTLETOE
December 1999
Silhouette Romance

N

MARIE FERRARELLA

Expecting... In Texas

Silhouette Books

Published by Silhouette Books
America's Publisher of Contemporary Romance

Special thanks and acknowledgment are given to Marie Ferrarella for her contribution to The Fortunes of Texas series.

 SILHOUETTE BOOKS

ISBN 0-373-65032-9

EXPECTING...IN TEXAS

Copyright © 1999 by Harlequin Books S.A.

Visit us at www.romance.net

Printed in U.S.A.

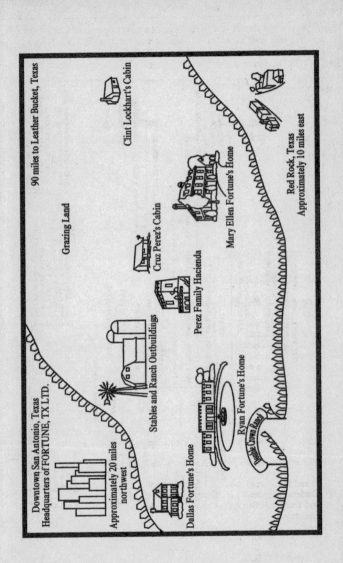

90 miles to Leather Bucket, Texas

Clint Lockhart's Cabin

Grazing Land

Cruz Perez's Cabin

Mary Ellen Fortune's Home

Perez Family Hacienda

Red Rock, Texas
Approximately 10 miles east

Downtown San Antonio, Texas
Headquarters of FORTUNE, TX LTD.

Stables and Ranch Outbuildings

Approximately 20 miles
northwest

Ryan Fortune's Home

Dallas Fortune's Home

THE FORTUNES OF TEXAS

KINGSTON FORTUNE (d)

1st marriage — PATIENCE TALBOT (d)

Teddy §

2nd marriage — SELENA HOBBS (d)

CAMERON (d) m MARY ELLEN LOCKHART

- HOLDEN ①
- LOGAN ⑤
- EDEN ⑦
  - m Lucinda Brightwater
  - Sawyer*

RYAN

1st marriage — JANINE LOCKHART (d)

- MATTHEW
- ZANE ⑫
  - m Claudia Beaumont
  - Bryan
- DALLAS ④
  - m Sara Andersen (d)
- VANESSA ②•••• VICTORIA ⑩
  - m Devin Kincaid

2nd marriage — SOPHIA BARNES

- CLINT LOCKHART brother of JACE LOCKHART ⑥

James a.k.a. Taylor

MIRANDA m Lloyd Carter (D)

- KANE
- GABRIELLE ⑧

LILY REDGROVE m Chester Cassidy (d)

- COLE* ⑪
- HANNAH ⑨
- MARIA

† ROSITA and RUBEN PEREZ

- Anita
- Carmen
- Frieda
- CRUZ ③
  - MAGGIE ④
    - m Craig Randall (D)
    - Travis

Key

- * Child of affair
- d Deceased
- D Divorced
- m Married
- ••• Twins
- † Affair
- § Kidnapped by maternal grandfather
- Loyal ranch staff

TITLES:

1. MILLION DOLLAR MARRIAGE
2. THE BABY PURSUIT
3. EXPECTING... IN TEXAS
4. A WILLING WIFE
5. CORPORATE DADDY
6. SNOWBOUND CINDERELLA
7. THE SHEIKH'S SECRET SON
8. THE HEIRESS AND THE SHERIFF
9. LONE STAR WEDDING
10. IN THE ARMS OF A HERO
11. WEDLOCKED?!
12. HIRED BRIDE

THE
FORTUNES
OF TEXAS™

 Meet the Fortunes of Texas

Cruz Perez: The carefree cowboy has never imagined himself as the baby-powder-and-diaper type, but honor demands he propose to the mother of his unborn child. Trouble is, the expectant beauty insists she doesn't want to become a wife....

Savannah Clark: The mom-to-be isn't eager to build a marriage for her baby's sake. She wants love—and is determined to show her cowboy how passion can lead to the promise of forever.

Rosita Perez: Everyone knows the Fortunes' housekeeper has a penchant for seeing the future. But when she envisions a connection between Maria Cassidy and the mysterious recovered baby, will anyone heed her premonition?

Maggie Perez Randall: The single mother has finally returned home to the bosom of her Texas family. Will the Double Crown Ranch be the place to make a new life for herself and her son?

To Melissa Jeglinski,
With love and appreciation

One

Her baby's father was here, somewhere, amid the throng of people who had turned out at the Double Crown Ranch to see Vanessa Fortune pledge her hand and her heart to the tall, good-looking FBI special agent Devin Kincaid.

Would there be a wedding like this for her someday? Savannah Clark wondered as she came to the end of her short journey down the aisle and stepped to the side. Would there be a man waiting for her someday, looking the way Devin did right at this moment? A little dazed, a little dazzled, and very much in love?

God, but she hoped so.

Just as Savannah turned and the Wedding March swelled, she saw him.

Cruz Perez had been looking at her. Their eyes met, touched, and she saw his smile. *Felt* his smile. That wide, sexy, scintillating smile that had made her lose her head, and perhaps her heart, for the space of a night three months ago at baby Bryan's christening party.

And perhaps, for even more than that.

Just as before, Cruz made her feel as if she were the only one there besides him. A very neat trick, considering just how many people had arrived at the ranch northwest of San Antonio to be crowded in neat rows of folding chairs set up before the altar. They were there to see the wedding of one of Ryan Fortune's twin daughters.

With a supreme effort, Savannah looked away from Cruz and toward the bride—her best friend from college. But she could still feel his intense gaze upon her. Color rose to her cheeks, but she kept her eyes riveted to the back of the house, where Vanessa was making her entrance.

Looking like a dapper, proud lion Ryan Fortune solemnly walked down the aisle with his daughter on his arm. But it was Vanessa who immediately stole everyone's attention, in her beautiful, form-fitting long white lace gown with its delicate Spanish lace veil that eloquently trailed after her. The handmade veil represented something borrowed as well as something old. Cruz's mother Rosita, the Fortune's housekeeper had worn it herself forty years ago, when she had married Ruben. It had been a gift to her from Vanessa's own mother, Janine Fortune—Ryan's late first wife.

Now it was a tradition, Savannah mused. A

lovely tradition. Vanessa would probably pass it on to her daughters when the time came.

And what would she pass on to her child? What sort of tradition could she give to a baby who was starting out life with only one parent, its very identity a secret that couldn't be shared?

Not now Savannah ordered herself sternly.

This wasn't the time for sad thoughts, only happy ones. She wished her hormones would stop swinging back and forth like a pendulum running amok, and just settle down to an even tempo. Pregnancy was making her lose her bearings; she wasn't accustomed to being like this.

Savannah stepped a little further to the side as Vanessa reached the altar that Cruz and his father had finished erecting only hours earlier. Vanessa gave up her bouquet to Savannah, a look filled with friendship and memories passing between them. Savannah was surprised to discover that Vanessa's fingertips were icy. She couldn't picture Vanessa afraid of anything.

Marriage was a big step and even if you were sure, you were still nervous, Savannah suddenly realized.

"Good luck," she mouthed. Vanessa brightened.

The soft buzzing behind them stopped, and the legion of guests fell silent as Reverend Callaway began to speak the words that would forever seal Vanessa and Devin to one another as husband and wife.

Savannah felt tears forming in the corners of her eyes as she listened to the precious vows—promises of a lifetime together. She remembered eyes that had made promises to her.

Promises that completely undid her that passionate, wonderful day, three months ago.

Savannah's mind had heard and understood the risks of falling for someone like Cruz. But her heart, well, her heart had been a completely different matter.

She tried to protect her heart now by holding back the memories, but they came anyway, like a flood that no barrier could hold at bay....

"Would you like to dance?"

Five simple words, tendered politely, that were destined to seal Savannah's fate. They had come floating to her, uttered by a voice that had just the smallest whisper of a Mexican accent.

All around her, couples were having a good time, dancing at Bryan Fortune's christening party. Savannah had always loved music, but had never had the time to learn how to dance. She was content now to stand on the sidelines and listen.

But she never got a chance to refuse Cruz. Even

as she turned around to face him, he was taking her hand in his and leading her to the dance floor that he had helped construct.

A small wave of panic swept through her. She hated looking like a fool. "Wait, I didn't say yes," she protested.

Facing her, Cruz was already taking her into his arms. "Oh, but you did. With your eyes." He fitted her body against his in a provocative move that was smoother than silk. Resting her hand against his chest, he smiled into her eyes. "I always pay very close attention to a lady's eyes. They tell me things she doesn't trust her mouth to say."

Savannah could feel her pulse accelerating and wondered if it was because of the wine she'd had, or the man she was with. For now, it was enough just to savor the thrill.

"Such as?"

The smile that curved his full, sensuous mouth cut clear down to her bones. "Such as—Yes, I would love to dance with you instead of standing here, only swaying to the music."

He was right, but she felt as if she had to protest. "I was not swaying."

His eyes laughed at her, and instantly she found herself being charmed. "Oh, but you were. I've been watching you for a while now."

She tried very hard not to be flattered but knew

that the effort was doomed to failure. After all, he could have been with anyone yet, he'd made his way to her without any encouragement on her part. She would have been less than human if some of the pride that her recent broken engagement had shredded so badly hadn't responded to that.

Even though she could feel electricity humming between them, she tried to keep the moment light. Amusement tugged at the corners of her mouth.

"Nothing better to do than to watch a woman keeping time to the music?"

Cruz leaned his head against hers. "Nothing."

He breathed the word so enticingly that every nerve ending along her body stood up in response. Savannah felt as if she were floating, not just across the floor, but all around. She felt as if everything within her had suddenly come awake again after a very long, troubled sleep.

Awake and aroused.

She struggled very hard to keep things in perspective, but even then she sensed she was doomed to lose.

They danced several dances together—danced and talked. With each new dance, he subtly moved her farther away from the crowd. And closer to him.

"Tell me, why does a lovely woman like you find herself alone at such a lavish party?"

"But I'm not alone." Feeling suddenly very light-headed, and maybe just a little giddy, she decided to play along and match Cruz, move for move, on a chessboard designed for sensuality and verbal foreplay. "I'm with you."

"Yes, yes, you are," he agreed heartily. "Perhaps I should have asked why you *arrived* alone." His eyes studied her for a fleeting second. "I seem to have touched something hurtful. I'm sorry."

God, what was the matter with her? A handsome hunk of a man was flirting with her, and she was letting her ex-fiancé Reese Culhane intrude and mess things up. Reese—who could look at her after she'd been with him for so long, after she'd given her heart to him, and say without a qualm that he'd fallen in love with someone else.

She shook her head. "You don't have anything to be sorry about. It's not your fault."

"Perhaps. But what I said reminded you of the wound, and for that, I apologize."

She'd come to the christening party to forget about Reese and the years she'd wasted loving him. He wasn't worth a memory, not now when she realized how very shallow he actually was.

Savannah placed her fingers to Cruz's lips, silencing his apology. "I don't want to talk about it."

His hand covering hers, he lightly kissed her fingertips. "Then we won't. We'll enjoy the music." He looked into her eyes so deeply that she was certain he'd touched her soul. "And the company."

Looking back later, Savannah knew that was the moment—the precise moment—when she fell completely under Cruz's spell. That was the moment when she decided to forget everything that troubled her—the heartache that had come along with her on this trip—so she could witness the christening of her best friend Vanessa's nephew. She made up her mind to live for the moment.

And the moment had been touched by Cruz.

"I've completely forgotten to introduce myself. I'm Cruz Perez," he whispered against her ear. And it was as if his very name was a magical cure to heal a heart that had been so badly misused.

Enjoying the warmth that shimmied up and down her spine, Savannah smiled to herself. "Yes, I know. I asked Vanessa about you. I'm Savannah Clark."

It wasn't a very sophisticated thing to admit. Saying it, Savannah fully expected Cruz to look at her like a male peacock whose vanity had been stroked. Instead, there had been an amused, partially obscured look in his eyes when he turned them on her.

As if her admission surprised him.

"You did?"

She nodded her head, excitement picking up pace. "Yes."

"And what is it she told you?" He cocked his head, waiting for her reply.

Vanessa's exact words came back to her. And looking at Cruz, Savannah could see why they had more than a kernel of truth to them. The man had incredibly disarming eyes and an equally disarming, wicked mouth.

"That mothers lock up their daughters when you're around."

He merely laughed at the warning. The sound wound its way deep into her system.

"Locked doors are really not an obstacle if someone is determined to get out." His eyes glinted with mischief and sensuality. "Or get in."

Looking into his eyes, Savannah had to remind herself to breathe. It took longer for her to find her tongue again.

"Vanessa says that you're the best horse trainer the ranch ever had," she said, abruptly steering the topic to safer ground. As she heard the words come out of her mouth, Savannah upbraided herself for sounding as stilted as a first-grade composition.

He smiled, looking over toward where Vanessa was standing. "Vanessa is known for her kind tongue."

Savannah was the first to agree that Vanessa had a huge heart. But she was also honest. "Yes, but she doesn't exaggerate." And Vanessa had been very adamant about Cruz's abilities—just as adamant about them as she'd been in her warning.

The band took a well-deserved break, and Savannah found herself alone with Cruz—farther away from the house than she'd realized.

It was as if the air had suddenly stopped moving around her, freezing everything except the two of them. Her eyes trapped by his, Savannah felt her heart hammering wildly.

As he leaned in to kiss her, she turned her head away at the last possible moment. She felt his lips brush against her hair. It was all she could do to take half a step back. Her mind scrambled for something to say. "Show them to me."

Cruz blinked. "Excuse me?"

Savannah swallowed. She probably sounded like a complete idiot. "Your horses. I'd like to see your horses."

Cruz paused, seeming to asses her motivation. "They aren't mine." He hesitated. "But maybe they're more mine than anyone's."

He took her hand in his. "You're not exactly dressed to go tramping through the stables."

When he looked at her like that, as if he knew

every thought in her head, every feeling in her heart, she found it difficult to think coherently.

"Dresses can be cleaned," she finally managed to get out.

His eyes washed over her slowly, making her warm, making her tremble inside—without so much as a word. And then, he laced his fingers through hers and turned away from the party.

And toward the stables.

"Well, what do you think?"

Hellfire was easily the most beautiful horse she had ever seen. It seemed fitting that the animal belonged to someone like Cruz. Both proud, magnificently regal—they belonged together. He told her that Vanessa had presented him with Hellfire for his twenty-fifth birthday.

Murmuring words of endearment, Savannah gently ran her hand along the horse's muzzle, stroking it. "I think she's beautiful."

Leaning against the stall, Cruz laughed. "It's a he, not a she. You can tell the difference by—"

"Yes," she said quickly, before Cruz felt called upon to go into an anatomy lesson. "I know exactly how to tell the difference. I was raised on a ranch."

Flustered, the color came rushing to her cheeks as she stepped away. It had been too crowded in the stall at first for her to clearly view the golden quarter horse. Now that she did, the gender was obvious.

His laughter continued. Savannah could feel her color deepen on her cheeks. "Don't laugh at me."

Guiding her away from Hellfire, Cruz drew her toward an empty stall. "Oh, but I'm not laughing at you. I'm laughing at how impossibly sweet and innocent you seem."

Stung, she raised her chin in protest. "I'm not innocent."

His laughter melted into a wide, sensuous smile. "Oh, excuse me. But of course, you're very worldly."

Her *parents* were worldly. In an effort to be less like them, she had avoided all their trappings. Maybe, in the long run, that left her a little naive.

She shrugged, looking away. "Well, all right, not very, but—"

He placed his hands on her shoulders, drawing her attention back to him. And the moment. Savannah lost the thread of her protest.

The wide smile was gone, replaced by a smaller, more intense one that curled her toes. With the tip of his finger, he toyed with a wisp of hair that fell against her cheek.

"And as a worldly woman, you wouldn't be offended if I kissed you?"

Was he asking for permission? Savannah's mouth went dry.

"If you—what?" she barely whispered.

His hands tightened ever so slightly on her shoulders as he brought her closer to him. "I prefer showing to talking."

She held her breath. Cruz slipped his hands from her shoulders up along the sides of her throat until his fingers gently framed her face. She felt every movement, vibrated with every heartbeat.

Waiting.

Anticipating.

This was so completely out of character for her that, for a brief moment, Savannah was convinced she was actually standing on the sidelines, watching, just like with the dance.

But she wasn't on the sidelines; she was in the heart of the dance. In the heart of the seduction as it unfurled around her, bit by heated bit.

She melted the moment his lips touched hers, a snowflake unable to keep its shape when it was blown into the path of a sunbeam.

The moan that escaped her lips was a sound of pure surrender.

He deepened the kiss, assaulting her mouth again and again. Savannah shivered as he tugged at the zipper that ran the length of her back. As he drew it all the way down, she felt the dress move away from her body.

And at that moment, she knew there was nothing she could refuse him.

Savannah couldn't get her bearings. Everything melted into everything else. The stable, the horses, the hay within the stall—all faded from her consciousness. All that there was, was Cruz. Cruz—with his thick, dark hair that flowed to almost the tops of his shoulders. Cruz—with his heartstopping smile, his deep brown eyes that undid her, and his hard, sleek body that quickened her pulse. Cruz—who had the ability to reduce her to a mass of molten desire.

She'd never behaved this way before, never abandoned herself, her common sense, her ethics before. She didn't believe in casual affairs—in casual anything, for that matter.

Yet here she was, giving herself to a man she'd only danced with. Wanting a man she'd barely met. Feeling as if she'd known him her entire life.

It made no sense. And yet, it was happening.

Each place he touched her quivering body seemed a revelation to her, leaving her bewildered, anticipating, yearning. Though not completely inexperienced, she knew she was merely a dazed novice at his hands. A novice with a thirst for learning.

He made her feel beautiful, like a queen beneath his hand, a wild woman beneath his questing mouth. It was as if every fiber of her body was on fire, and he was fanning the flames.

Explosions racked her body as Cruz skillfully moved his fingers, his lips and his tongue over her. There were points along her body she'd thought harmless, certainly not centers of passion.

Until now.

The skin behind her knees, the space inside her elbow, the hollow of her throat—all these he teased, all these he turned into places of heated desire. And when he moved lower, when he finally drove himself into her, she thought herself too weak, too spent to react.

She was wrong.

Everything that came before was but a warm-up act for a finale that left Savannah sobbing his name, biting her lower lip for fear of screaming and bringing everyone here—to this stable where she felt reborn.

"I now pronounce you husband and wife."

The words uttered by the minister abruptly drew Savannah back to the wedding. What was wrong with her? This was Vanessa's moment. She was here to share it with her, not relive one night of passion best forgotten.

Two

"You came back."

Only ten minutes into the wedding reception, Savannah's stomach merged with her heart and both instantly raced for her throat. She wasn't sure just which won the narrow space for its own as she turned around to face Cruz for the first time since that heated encounter in the stables.

Dressed in a black, embroidered western jacket and a light blue shirt that made his complexion that much more romantically olive, Cruz was standing behind her, a glass of punch in each hand.

It must have been her stomach that won the race, Savannah reasoned. Because her heart had stopped. Completely.

Cruz nodded toward the glasses, his smile unfurling like warm brandy sipped slowly on a cold day. "I seem to find myself with two glasses. Would you like to help me out and take one?"

She became aware that she was smiling in return. Widely. Savannah reminded herself that there was absolutely no reason for her to behave like a tongue-tied adolescent. Yes, he was beautiful, and yes, they had made wild, wonderful, passionate love together. But in the greater scheme of things, that meant nothing.

Nothing, except that their night of lovemaking had produced a baby. A baby she wasn't ever going to let Cruz know was his. Because she would never tie him to her. Not with bonds—like her parents—forged out of guilt.

Savannah inclined her head as she took the glass. "I guess I could, just this once."

She looked at the way the red punch caught the sun within it and gleamed invitingly. Almost as invitingly as Cruz's eyes had that night.

And now.

She raised her eyes to his. "And why wouldn't I come back for my best friend's wedding?"

"No reason." He shrugged. His eyes traveled over the soft contours of her face. Savannah felt as if he were actually touching her. "Except that you left so quickly the last time we were together. When I woke, you were gone. I thought that perhaps it was something I'd said. Or done."

His smile was so sensual that she struggled to keep her mind on the conversation.

Yes, it was something you'd done. You completely unraveled me, made me behave so that I didn't even recognize myself. And then made me want more.

Savannah took a long sip before she spoke, her throat suddenly too parched to house dust.

"I had to get back." She purposely looked past his head as she spoke. "I had papers to grade. It was the end of the semester—the end of the year," she corrected, silently chastising herself for stumbling.

But while she'd always been very self-assured in her chosen professional life as an elementary school teacher, her personal one, especially since Reese had left, was another matter entirely. Even before Reese had broken her heart by breaking off their engagement, she had never been very experienced when it came to men.

That was probably why he'd strayed and ultimately left, she had come to realize. Because she wasn't exciting enough to hold him. All he'd wanted, apparently, was a woman who was as empty of mind as she was well endowed of body.

But Savannah had always been praised more for her mind than her looks. She was not the type who instantly attracted men. That was part of the reason she'd been so flattered by Cruz and his attention. He could have had any woman—and there had been plenty at the party. Yet he'd singled her out.

She couldn't help wondering why.

"Good." Pleased, he nodded his head. "Then it wasn't me. What about now?"

She didn't understand. "Now?"

"Will you be leaving tomorrow?" He raised one eyebrow, as if he could see right through her excuse, right through *her*. "More papers to grade?"

Was he asking her because he wanted to be sure that she wouldn't be around to become a problem? Or was he asking because he wanted to know whether she'd grown up a little, become a little more sophisticated?

Savannah couldn't make up her mind which it was. Not when she was being so distracted by the look in his eyes, by the way his lips moved when he spoke. There was no doubt about it—Cruz Perez was raw sex and sensuality, served up on a section of delicious toast.

It was a crisp September afternoon. There was even a bit of a chill in the wind. Yet she felt so warm, as if the air around her were heated by his presence.

It took a moment, but she finally found her voice, and with it a little bit of conviction. "No, no papers to grade."

"Oh. Right. It's too early." He looked at her knowingly. "You're one of the nice teachers."

"One of the nice teachers?" she echoed, not sure what he was driving at. Was he referring to some sort of exclusive club? Whatever it was, he'd called her nice, and she liked that. Liked thinking that he'd meant it. "What makes you say that?"

"Instinct," he said, sounding sincere.

His mother was the "seer" around here, the one who had dreams she claimed came true. It was only so in about a third of the cases, although no one went out of their way to point the fact out to her. But even so, if there was a scrap of truth about her abilities, maybe they were passed on. Maybe he'd inherent a smattering of it himself. Because he was beginning to sense things about Savannah Clark, things that he found enticing and pleasing.

Casually, Cruz threaded his arm around her shoulders.

He had no way of knowing how intimate that felt to her, Savannah thought. Or maybe he did, and that was the whole point of it. She struggled not to enjoy the feeling as much as she did. Allowing herself to venture deeper into the trap really wouldn't help anything in the long run.

But logic didn't seem to be working for her today, she thought. Magic was. His magic.

"I always used to hate it when the teachers would give long assignments the first week of school," he confided. "I couldn't shake the feeling that they did it to get back at us because they had to return from their vacations and work again."

Habit made her protective of her vocation. "That's not true. It's to get students back into a thinking mode after they've been playing all summer." And Savannah didn't have to ask to know that Cruz had been one of those students who had played the hardest and the longest.

"There's nothing wrong with playing." His mouth curved a little more deeply, drawing her in further still. "It can be hard work, too."

Not for him, she thought. For him, it came naturally. Like breathing. Like kissing.

"Maybe you're right."

His face turned toward hers, Cruz lightly touched the outline of her pearl drop earring and sent it swaying ever so slightly.

"So," he asked softly, "you like to stimulate your students?"

Her blood was beginning to roar through her veins, like Indy-500 stock cars revving up their engines. She had to concentrate on each word to get it out.

"Getting them to think for themselves is always a good thing."

He smiled to himself, seeing the effect he was having on her. That it heightened his own excitement was a bonus in the bargain.

"And you are an expert on that?" he teased. "On thinking?"

Her knees felt like water. Which made her knees and her mind a perfect set.

Savannah licked her lips. "Not an expert, but—"

She stopped. Cruz was making her feel flustered, and he knew it. She could tell by the look in his eyes. Why couldn't she resist him? Why couldn't she be sophisticated like Vanessa or one of her other friends, and just exchange teasing phrases?

He moved slightly to stand in front of her, his brown eyes challenging her. "Tell me, Savannah, what am I thinking now?"

He'd never called her by her name before. It seemed to float to her on his tongue, making her feel even warmer than she already was. She was beginning to wish fervently that the bridesmaid dress had been sleeveless instead of having tight, long sleeves that ended a little over her wrists. She had a feeling even that wouldn't help to cool her off.

After a moment, she found her breath. "That you'd like to dance with me." It was a stab in the dark, and probably wrong, but it was the only thing that came to her.

The deep, lusty laugh enveloped her as Cruz obviously enjoyed her answer.

That was definitely not what had been on his mind. He was thinking of the way she'd looked, with only the moonlight sneaking into the stables. She'd looked soft and pliant, with the sheen of lovemaking still fresh on her firm, nude body and seeing her like that had made him want to make love to her all over again.

"All right," he agreed amiably. "We can do that if you'd like."

She'd been right. Dancing hadn't been on his mind. But she was afraid to think what had been. Afraid to think because she might be right.

More afraid because she might be wrong—and disappointed.

Taking the glass from her hand, Cruz placed it on the first available flat surface, then gently took her into his arms.

She tried not to let the warmth of Cruz's body seep into hers. She might as well have tried to breathe under water. It couldn't be done.

Savannah felt like a princess, just like the first time they had danced.

"I looked for you, you know. The morning after," he added when she looked up at him questioningly. "I was surprised that you had gone so quickly."

She'd gone because the reality of what she had done had suddenly hit her with the force of a two-ton truck. She'd been embarrassed and somewhat ashamed, as well. And more than that, she'd been afraid that he would laugh at her, at how easily he'd been able to seduce her. She couldn't have faced his laughter. Better to walk away with a lovely memory than to deal with aftermath and reality.

Except that now she *had* to.

She studied his face, looking for an answer, trying not to let herself be distracted. "Why would you look for me?"

"Why does any man look for a woman?"

She lifted one shoulder beneath her gown in a half shrug. "For a very long list of reasons," she murmured evasively as he spun her around.

"Shorten it," he whispered against her hair.

Urges began to grow, to multiply within her.

No, not this time, Savannah warned silently, trying hard to steel herself. She couldn't allow herself to give in again.

No matter what she wanted, she had to maintain a barrier. Otherwise, she wouldn't be able to stay here. And the Double Crown was her last hope. She'd been "released" from Pierce Academy after the principal had discovered she was pregnant. Out of sympathy and kindness, Vanessa had offered her a job and a place to stay at the ranch for as long as she wanted it.

Savannah had no other options. She absolutely refused to turn to either of her parents. They had already done enough for her by getting married in the first place to give her a name. For that, they'd each paid dearly and continually suffered one another's company in a union that should never have been allowed to take place. She'd left home as soon as she was old enough, unable to stand the guilt of knowing she'd inadvertently ruined two people's lives just by drawing breath.

It was a fate she was determined that she was never going to bequeath to her child.

Putting on her most carefree face, Savannah turned it up to him. "Is it your sworn duty to seduce every woman under the age of fifty?"

He saw the smile playing on her lips and realized she was teasing rather than being coy. With Savannah, there was a difference.

"Only the beautiful ones."

"Oh, I see." Beautiful. It was a word she'd never heard applied to herself, and she didn't cleave to it now. "Then you're just practicing on me."

"Practicing?" For a second, Cruz didn't understand, then he realized that perhaps she was being coy after all. "*Querida,* I don't need practice. And you are the prize."

She laughed shortly. She'd been an ugly duckling as a child, a fact that only added to her parents' misery. Neither could believe that they had created such a plain child between them, when they were both regarded as extremely good-looking in their circles.

"I'm hardly that."

He cocked his head, looking at her. "You don't think you're beautiful?"

The subject made her uncomfortable. She'd heard enough taunts as a child to instinctively brace herself for a punch line at her expense. "I don't think about the way I look at all."

"It's a lie." Cruz called her on it, looking amused. "Every woman thinks about how she looks—if she is exciting, if she makes a man's head turn, his mouth water, his—"

Savannah was afraid to let him go any further. "I don't."

His eyes narrowed. "Then you are even more unique than I thought."

He doesn't think I'm unique—it's a line, she told herself.

A line she wished with all her heart she could believe.

Becoming defensive, Savannah raised her chin ever so slightly.

"I'm not unique, I'm stable. Sensible." She ticked off terms that she'd heard applied to herself over the course of her life.

Cruz made a face at the last word. "Sensible is for shoes."

He made it sound as if it were a bad thing. She didn't think so. Maybe it wasn't a very exciting quality, but she was proud of being sensible—even though what she had done that night in the stable was as far from sensible as the earth was from the moon.

"Not if you work for a living."

Savannah had struck a chord. Cruz looked at her thoughtfully for a long moment as they whirled around on the floor.

"Maybe you are at that. Sensible," he added in case she'd lost the thread. "But you are still beautiful," he insisted.

"It's the dress."

"You can put a beautiful gown on a warthog," he pointed out. "But in the long run, you still have a very ugly animal in a dress."

She laughed. "You're very colorful."

If the compliment pleased him, he gave no indication. "I read."

The admission caught her interest, appealing to the teacher within her. "A lot?"

He shrugged, perhaps uncomfortable at the confession. "Whenever I get the chance."

It wasn't something he often admitted, but he read everything he could get his hands on, determined not to just work with his hands, but with his mind as well. He couldn't afford to go to college, the way Ryan Fortune's children had, but that didn't mean he couldn't continue learning.

He looked around at the others dancing around them. "I want to know as much as these *hidalgos* do. More." That was the whole point of it. They took their education for granted, something that was handed to them. To him, knowledge was a special thing, even if he didn't readily talk about it.

"*Hidalgos?*"

"It means—"

"I know what it means," she interrupted, wanting to get at the heart of his feelings before he changed the subject. "Do you see them that way? The Fortunes?"

He began to laugh off his words, then stopped abruptly. Maybe the role of the smiling, easygoing cowboy was getting to him. God knows he was tired of it, of its confining web.

"There is no other way to see them. Some are kinder than others, to be sure, but all of them see themselves as above the people who work for them." Chunks of memories crowd his mind. Memories that weren't always pleasant. Memories that would probably surprise someone like Savannah Clark with her education and her upper crust private school. "When I was growing up, my mother took care of the Fortune children, and my sisters and I played with them. But their father made sure that none of us would ever forget that there was a line between us." Bitterness infused his smile. "Master and servant."

"But Vanessa's not like that," Savannah protested. She couldn't picture Vanessa ever putting anyone in their so-called place. Especially not because of the whimsy of fate and financial circumstances. And Vanessa's brother Dallas wasn't like that, either. She knew that for a fact.

"No," Cruz agreed. "She is not. But she is different from them." He looked pointedly at Savannah. "And different from me." After a small pause, a smile teased his mouth. "Come, this is far too serious a topic for a wedding, and you are here to have fun."

But her eyes held his. "That doesn't mean I can't learn something."

"Maybe we can both learn something," he remarked playfully as he whirled her around the floor once more.

Savannah had the uneasy feeling that she'd just been put on notice.

Three

"Mind if I cut in?"

Cruz looked over his shoulder to see Dallas Fortune standing behind him on the dance floor.

It was on the tip of his tongue to say, yes, he did mind. Because it was, Cruz swallowed the words, a little disturbed that they should have been the ones to rise in response. After all, it wasn't as if he had any claims on Savannah, or even wanted any. She had just aroused his interest—temporarily.

They'd spent the last few hours together, dancing and talking. He had to admit that he hadn't realized just how much time he had spent in her company; it had passed so quickly. They had even discussed his plans for a ranch of his own, something he wasn't in the habit of talking about with anyone outside the family. Even with his family, he remained guarded, using his words sparingly.

But talking to Savannah had been different. Easy. The plans, the dreams, had somehow just been coaxed out by the expression on her face, the light in her eyes.

He'd talked too much. It was high time for him to turn his attention elsewhere, Cruz decided. There were a great many other attractive single women at the party besides Savannah.

There was really no reason for him to stagnate here. No reason at all.

"Be my guest." Cruz released Savannah's hand from his and stepped away, giving Dallas a clear field.

His intention was to turn immediately away and seek out the first pretty, unattached woman he came across. But something held him where he was. He watched as Dallas slipped his hand around Savannah's waist and drew her to him.

A strange, hot feeling rose quickly in Cruz's chest. He waited for it to fall back down, to fizzle out.

When it didn't on its own, Cruz banked it down, and was surprised at the effort it took. He didn't know just what the hell was going on, but he wasn't about to waste time mulling over it.

He looked around—everywhere but where Dallas and Savannah were dancing—searching for his next companion. Seeing a woman who he thought might provide him with a little diversion, Cruz lost no time crossing to her.

Looking in his direction, the woman smiled a warm invitation.

Cruz returned it. He was glad Dallas had come along to free him up when he did. Maybe Cruz had lost track of time there for a little while, but he was back on track now. It was way past time to change partners.

The song was slow, and Savannah let herself drift with it. The tingling sensation had disappeared. At least her body would have a chance to get back to normal, now that Cruz was no longer holding her.

She rested her head against Dallas's shoulder. Vanessa's older brother had always been kind to her, and she liked him. When she and Vanessa had attended college together and Dallas had come up for visits, he'd always made a point of treating her as if she were his sister, too. It had earned him a permanent soft spot in her heart.

"Are you having a good time?" His voice drifted into the contented haze forming around her.

Savannah didn't bother lifting her head. "Very." For perhaps the first time in three months, she mused. Since the last time she'd been here.

"I wanted to make sure you weren't overwhelmed by everything."

Savannah raised her head to look at him. "Overwhelmed?"

Dallas nodded. "We Fortunes have a habit of steamrollering over people—quite unintentionally. Vanessa tells me that you'll be staying on at the ranch as a bookkeeper."

How much did he know about that? Self-conscious, Savannah looked away, avoiding his eyes.

She saw Cruz dancing with another woman. Disappointment mushroomed through her even as she tried to subdue it. Cruz was free to do whatever he wanted, be with whomever he wanted. She had no claims on him. None, at any rate, that she was willing to make.

"Yes, that's right."

"Vanessa didn't talk you into it, did she?"

The question caught her attention, and Savannah looked at him, puzzled. "What do you mean?"

Dallas laughed softly. "Well, I know you're a teacher at that private school. Pierce Academy, isn't it?"

So he didn't know that she'd been asked to leave. Relieved, Savannah nodded. This put an entirely different light on the conversation.

"I just wanted to be sure that Vanessa hadn't twisted your arm to get you to agree to work on the ranch. I know she wasn't happy that you were so far away." He smiled at her. "She missed you a lot."

It was nice to know that someone did. Savannah supposed it was the state she found herself in, but of late she'd felt part misfit, part outcast—and completely vulnerable.

"And I've missed her," she confided. A smile bloomed as she looked up at him. He really did act like a big brother sometimes. She appreciated that the way only an only child could. "That's very sweet of you, Dallas, worrying about me. But Vanessa didn't talk me into anything. There have been...cutbacks at the school," she said evasively. Right now, she didn't really feel like admitting the truth. She'd have to deal with that soon enough if things worked out and she remained. "I just discovered that I was being let go a few hours before I flew out. Your sister was kind enough to offer me a position here. Luckily, I had some bookkeeping experience in college."

One song ended and another, its tempo much quicker, began. Dallas gave no indication that he was about to retreat. Instead, his step quickened in time to the music as he swept her around the floor.

"Kind, nothing." He laughed at the thought. "If you work at the Double Crown Ranch, I guarantee you'll earn your pay. My father doesn't let anyone coast along, not even his own kids. *Especially* his own kids," Dallas amended. But there was no bitterness in his voice. "A little hard work never killed anyone, but I did want you to know what you were getting yourself into."

"Information duly noted," Savannah said, growing a little breathless. Dallas was far more taken with the execution of fancy footwork than Cruz, had been. With Cruz she'd been more aware of bodies moving than flying feet.

He looked down at her face. "In that case, may I be the first to welcome you aboard, Savannah. We'll be seeing a lot of each other. I've had to temporarily move back into my father's house while my roof damage is being repaired."

The room began to spin just a little, and she held onto his arm as much for support as for form. "I'm sorry about your house, though it will be nice to spend some time with you. But don't I have to get approved by your father, first before the bookkeeping job is officially mine?"

Dallas shook his head. "Just technically. Nothing more than rubber-stamping at this stage," he assured her. "He trusts Vanessa's judgment. We all do."

"Then I guess I'm hired." One huge weight off her shoulders, she thought. At least for the time being. The rest of the future was just going to have to take care of itself.

As the pace picked up again, Dallas glided her around another couple. "I guess you are."

Savannah was smiling at Dallas. Now she was laughing at something he'd just said. Cruz found himself taking in every movement. The woman in his arms was vivacious and had eyes only for him, but he was oblivious to her and her blatant attempts to snare his interest.

His attention was on the couple across the floor. His grip on the woman's hand tightened slightly as he watched Dallas bend his head and whisper something into Savannah's ear. She laughed in response, the sound muted by the music. Cruz heard it in his head, anyway.

What the hell were they talking about?

Again he found that he had to bank down the strange, hot feelings that threatened to take control of him. He muttered an oath under his breath, turning his partner so that he could get a better view of Savannah and her companion.

"What's the matter, darlin'?" the woman purred. "You look like your mind's a million miles away."

Cruz looked at his partner. The lopsided grin that followed covered a thousand transgressions. "Just thinking of you and the night ahead, Gia."

The blonde snuggled against him, her sigh warm on his chest. "Tell me more."

Watching Cruz and the blonde who hermetically adhered herself to his body, Savannah struggled not to let a new wave of sadness engulf her. For now, things were as good as they could get. Better than she'd hoped.

She was just going to have to content herself with that.

Savannah had no idea why she couldn't.

Pride filled Rosita Perez's ample bosom as she watched Vanessa dance on the arm of her new husband. It was the kind of pride a mother might feel on the day of her daughter's wedding. The kind of pride Rosita had felt watching her own daughters when they were married.

Her body swaying ever so slightly in time with the music, Rosita continued watching from the sidelines. Vanessa Fortune might as well have been her daughter. She had helped raise the girl and her twin sister, Victoria, from the time both were babies. She'd stepped in on a full-time basis when the twins' mother, Janine, had died, filling the huge gap as best she could so that the Fortune children would always know that there was someone around who cared for them.

Ryan Fortune did care, of course, she thought as

she helped herself to a small canapé, but he was only a man, and men were inept when it came to showing their feelings for their children. And then, of course, he'd made the mistake of marrying that woman, Sophia. His second wife had gotten her hooks into him, and the children had become more Rosita's than ever.

Rosita delicately wiped her mouth with a napkin. Even her husband Ruben could have shown his feelings more, although he was better than most. No, in her generation it was the women who felt, the women who cried and encouraged and guided. It had always been second nature to her.

Rosita only hoped that she'd infused some of her values into the current generation of Fortunes, so they would be freer to show their feelings, freer to love those who deserved loving.... Like this small baby whom God had directed into their home, Rosita mused as she looked toward the ornate bassinet that was butted up against the side of one of the banquet tables.

When Claudia and Matthew had discovered that the baby whom Devin and Vanessa had rescued wasn't their own precious kidnapped Bryan, they had taken it upon themselves to care for the little mystery baby. Taylor, as they were calling him, had the hereditary crown-shaped birthmark, thus proving he was indeed a Fortune. The only trouble was that none of the Fortune men had claimed responsibility for fathering the little angel. Regardless, the family had come to love the boy in the short time he'd been with them.

The bassinet could be seen from anywhere in the room. Afraid of a repetition of the awful kidnapping at the christening, Matthew and Claudia had made certain that the baby remained well in sight during the whole reception. They didn't want to lose him, and perhaps lose the only real connection they still had to their own lost son. Though the FBI and Sheriff Grayhawk were still working on finding the kidnappers and baby Bryan, all leads were cold. At least the media weren't hounding the Fortunes; the story was being kept quiet out of fear of tabloid exploitation.

Still, Rosita knew the kidnapping was placing a serious strain on Matthew and Claudia's marriage. They'd moved back into Ryan's home, and Rosita saw them daily. She could cut the tension between them with a knife.

Poor lamb, Rosita thought looking down at the baby. *Who is it you really belong to?*

Filled with sympathy for the child, for his real mother, who could be desperately searching for him even now, and for Matthew and Claudia and their continuous anguish, Rosita made her way over to the bassinet.

She noted that Lily Cassidy, Ryan Fortune's long-lost love, and Lily's daughter, Maria, were already there. Lily and Ryan had been lovers once. Lily had recently reentered Ryan's life and the difference in the man could be seen instantly. About time the man was happy again, Rosita thought. She noticed that the baby began to fret as she approached. Rosita saw Maria lift the baby and take him into her arms with a practiced ease. Usually rebellious and embittered, Maria seemed oddly self-confident as she held the child. The baby quieted instantly.

Rosita paused, studying the younger woman.

Seeing her, Lily smiled a greeting to Rosita. "You must be very proud." Her eyes indicated Vanessa.

Rosita nodded. Lily was a fine lady, and genteel in the traditional sense of the word. Lily understood that Vanessa was like a daughter to her. Ryan would do well to make her his wife, Rosita mused. Lily would undoubtedly bring honor and style to the family.

Not like Sophia. She'd never been a Fortune—not truly.

"She does make a beautiful bride," Rosita agreed with genuine pride. "And more than that, she is a beautiful person." She looked at Maria and the baby. "Would you like me to take him for a little while? That way you and Ms. Lily can feel free to have a good time."

Maria merely scowled in response.

"That's very sweet of you, Rosita," Lily responded, covering for her daughter's rudeness. Lily rose from her chair. "I guess it doesn't take all of us to guard one small baby." She passed her hand lightly over the infant's downy head. There was affection in her eyes when she looked at Taylor.

Rosita saw a strange expression pass over Maria's face as Lily spoke. It looked suspiciously like fear. Was she worried about the baby, too? Everyone at the ranch had fallen in love with this little waif, who laughed and already seemed to have a zest for life. But it was out of character for Maria to care about anyone, even a small baby.

"Perhaps a little of both." Rosita reached for the baby, but Maria stepped back, unwilling to relinquish her hold. Rosita looked at her quizzically.

"That's all right, I don't mind," Maria said quickly. "I like holding him, and he seems to be happy right now. Why don't you just go and enjoy yourselves?" It was more of a dismissal than a suggestion.

Lily pressed her lips together. "Maria, you really should get out and mingle a little. I was hoping that—"

Maria's face clouded over. "Yes, Mother, I know exactly what you were hoping." Her eyes strayed toward Matthew before she turned her back on her mother. Her attention became centered on the baby. "But I'm happy here, just holding the baby. Why can't you just accept that?"

Rosita looked away, embarrassed for Lily and not wanting to cause her any further discomfort. Her own daughters would never speak to her this way, especially not in front of someone else. It seemed a shame that such a fine lady like Lily had to put up with such rude behavior.

"I had better see if they have enough wine." Rosita nodded toward some of the trays scattered about on the surrounding tables. "It looks as if we are gathering too many empty glasses."

"Oh, there you are." Coming up behind Lily, Ryan slipped his arms around her, hugging her to him. "I haven't had a chance to claim a dance with you in the last hour. Baxter Cordell is talking my ear off about some infernal idea. Something about a dude ranch, of all things. Come save me," he urged the woman who shared his heart and his bed, and would someday soon, God willing, share his name as well.

Turning around in his arms so that she faced him, Lily pretended to sigh. "All right, if I must."

Some of the tension began to leave her brow as she let Ryan lead her away.

"I saw you hovering by Taylor." Ryan curled her hand in his.

"Just being wistful," Lily admitted. She looked back toward her daughter holding the baby. It made for a pretty picture. "I can't wait until one of the children makes me a grandmother."

Ryan laughed and shook his head. "You're far too young looking, Lily, for anyone to think of you as a grandmother."

Her laughter, light and airy, mingled with his. "That's part of the joy of it."

Rosita looked thoughtfully over at Maria. *Perhaps you already are one.*

It was 3:30 a.m. All the guests had gone. Darkness and quiet enveloped the Fortune family home. Bolting upright, Rosita cried out in surprised anguish before her eyes opened to admit the darkness within her bedroom.

Lying beside her, Ruben roused himself. Though he was not a stranger to these kinds of outbursts from his wife in the middle of the night, it took him a moment to orient himself and pull himself together.

Half asleep, still lying in bed, he managed to

thread his arms around her waist. "Shh, Rosita, it was just a bad dream."

"Yes," she agreed breathlessly, her pulse still beating erratically. "No," she declared suddenly, as things began to focus in her brain. "Not a bad dream, an omen. A sign." Excited, breathless, she shifted, looking at her husband. His eyes were half closed. Rosita shook him by the shoulder. "It was a sign."

Ruben opened his eyes reluctantly. "What are you talking about?"

It was all still jumbled in her head, but bits and pieces were becoming clearer. A feeling of urgency filled her, although she didn't know why. "I dreamed that Lily was nursing a baby."

"What baby?"

"I'm not sure."

Ruben turned on his side. His arm under his pillow, he snuggled against it. He was anxious to get a little more sleep before dawn and hard work met him. "That's nice."

Upset by his reaction, Rosita leaned over her husband, talking directly into his ear. "Don't you want to hear the rest of the dream?"

Ruben struggled against irritation and tried to maintain his hold on sleep. "Why would I want to hear what indigestion has made you dream of?"

He was always blaming her visions on indigestion. But he was a man and knew little about things like visions. "Not indigestion." She shook his shoulder again. "Listen to me, old man."

He sighed, knowing that he was waging a losing battle. But he was bound to try anyway.

"The middle of the night is the time for sleeping, not listening." His eyes shut, he willed her into silence—as if that ever worked. "I will listen in the morning." When he fervently hoped all this nonsense of hers would be forgotten. He supposed that made him a bit of a dreamer, too.

But Rosita was determined to talk about her dream now, while the pieces were all still fresh in her mind. "I was watching Maria with the baby at the wedding today."

More awake than asleep now, Ruben sighed again. "You had nothing better to occupy yourself with?" he mumbled into his pillow.

She ignored the question. "The baby seemed to recognize Maria."

Ruben turned toward her. This had to stop. He couldn't sleep if she insisted on talking. "How could he recognize anyone? He is only, what? Three months old perhaps? And besides, he has been here for only a few weeks."

Vindicated, Rosita held up a finger for emphasis. "That is my point."

She had lost him. It was nothing new. Ruben

had learned a long time ago not to try to keep up with the way his wife's mind worked. It only led to frustration in the end.

"Your point is dull, my love. Now, please, for the love of our children, let me get some sleep before I fall off my horse tomorrow."

He was turning away from her. In a moment, she knew he would be asleep. The man was infuriating. "But you haven't heard my dream yet."

Ruben sighed again, louder this time. It was a sigh of resignation, if not surrender. There was no talking her out of it.

"All right." Turning, he faced her squarely, his eyes wide open—the way they probably would remain for the rest of what was left of the night, he thought mournfully. "Tell me your dream and then maybe we'll both get some sleep." Although he sincerely doubted it.

Victorious, Rosita proceeded slowly now, for effect and drama. "I dreamed that Lily was nursing a baby." She paused significantly. "Suddenly, the baby transformed into a scorpion and stung her!"

"Definitely indigestion," Ruben pronounced. Having done his duty, he turned away from her again. "All right, you have told me. Now let's get some sleep."

Disappointed, Rosita glared at him. What did

she expect? He was a man and didn't understand these things. "You are impossible."

"No, only tired."

The sentence came out in a soft sigh. Ruben was asleep before the last word was out of his mouth, leaving Rosita to lie beside him, upset and fuming.

And convinced that her vision contained more than an ounce of truth....

"Are you sure?" Cruz looked at his sister, surprised and maybe just a little more pleased than he wanted to let on, even to himself. Maggie had come knocking on his door this morning with the news just as he was about to head toward the stable.

It had stopped him in his tracks.

Maggie grinned at her older brother. So, she'd been right. There *was* something going on between Cruz and Vanessa's friend. Watching him last night, she'd sensed that something was up, but she hadn't been sure until just this moment.

"Of course I'm sure." She fell into step with him as he went to get his horse.

"Do you know how long she'll be staying?"

Cruz's curiosity tickled her. He'd always been so very fickle before, going through women like a man leafing slowly through the pages of a magazine. This time, it looked as if he'd stopped to read the story that went along with the pictures.

About time, Maggie thought.

Cruz had spent the better part of the reception in Savannah Clark's company. That had to mean something since he normally divided his time with no less than five women during the course of one of these parties.

But to say so, Maggie knew, would be to annoy him. She decided to save that little observation as ammunition for some future time. She never knew when she might need it.

"Indefinitely." Maggie watched Cruz saddle his horse, his face impassive. She knew him better than that. He wouldn't be asking questions if he wasn't interested. He wasn't one for idle gossip. "It seems the school where she was teaching had to let some of their staff go. She needed a job and Vanessa offered her one. She'd going to be the ranch's new bookkeeper."

So, she'd be working for the Fortunes. That put her on the same level as he was. Cruz wondered if Savannah thought of that as a step down. He knew from experience that the Fortune family and their hired help did not readily mix, no matter what magnanimous words might be said to the contrary or what invitations were extended. The bottom line was that the Fortunes were above them and would always continue that way.

Tightening the saddle cinch, he looked at his sister. "So she'll be staying on."

Maggie nodded. "Looks that way." Maggie made no attempt to hide the fact that she was taken with his reaction. "Are you interested?"

Yes, he thought, he was interested. For all her shyness, Savannah had been a very satisfying lover and he wanted to lure her back to his bed. Just to assure himself that he'd over-glorified the night in his mind.

But he'd missed his chance to find out last night. After Dallas had cut in on them, other members of the Fortune family had followed and gone on to monopolize Savannah's time. So he had distracted himself with the woman he'd been with.

Or tried to. But his heart hadn't been in it and he'd gone back to his cabin alone, to fall into a restless sleep that had left him more tired than refreshed when he woke up this morning.

The tangle of dreams he'd had had faded the moment he'd woken up, but they had left him weary. And more restless.

"Are you interested?" Maggie repeated, peering at his face.

Cruz shrugged, absently looking over toward the house. "No more than usual," he finally said.

But Maggie had her doubts about that.

Four

Vanessa and Devin left on their honeymoon immediately after the reception, and life on the sprawling ranch went back to normal.

But normal did not really include her, Savannah thought as she sat the next morning in the dining room, pretending to eat breakfast. She'd gone from being Vanessa's best friend to being a ranch employee, and wasn't really sure anymore how to behave.

Dallas was at the table with her, as was Ryan. After murmuring a preoccupied hello in her direction, Ryan had been prodded by his son to give the final okay on Savannah's hiring.

"Hmm? Oh yes, of course. I'm sure you'll be fine." Picking up the cup of coffee at his place, he began walking away with it, heading for the front door. "But there's no need to rush into anything," he tossed back at her in his wake, still preoccupied. "Why don't you wait until Vanessa returns before you get started? Just consider this an extended vacation for now."

Translation: I'm being retained as a favor, Savannah thought. There was no reason to wait for Vanessa. Vanessa was a psychologist, not the manager of the ranch. That position belonged to Ryan, and to Dallas in part because Dallas would be the one who'd be taking over the ranch when his father retired.

A sour taste formed in Savannah's mouth. She'd told Vanessa that she didn't like the idea of being anyone's charity case.

Dallas waited until he heard the front door close before saying anything to Savannah. "It's not what you think."

Savannah stopped toying with the breakfast pastry on her plate. There was just no way she could bring it to her mouth. She'd spent the first half hour of her day being miserably ill with morning sickness. "What do you mean?"

"I mean that Vanessa didn't make up the bookkeeping job. We really do need someone to keep the books around here." He looked toward the front of the house. "It's just that lately, Dad's been kind of preoccupied. What with the divorce, and Sophia trying to take him for all he's worth."

Savannah knew all about the bitter battle Ryan Fortune was embroiled in. "You read minds?"

Dallas laughed, shaking his head. "Your face is an open book. Consider yourself on salary as of this morning.'' He pushed back from the table. "As for the books, I'll show them to you myself later this week. I work at the Fortune TX offices in town, but I also have a hand in the ranch management. For now, why don't you do what Dad said? Just enjoy our hospitality. Go for a ride. I'll even join you, if you like."

Savannah gave the pastry one last look and then rose from the table. "No, you've been kind enough already. I think I could use a little time to myself right now, if you don't mind."

He understood very well about wanting to be alone. Ever since his wife had died, Dallas had carved out huge chunks of solitude for himself.

"Understood." Finished, Dallas dropped his napkin beside his plate and rose. "Tell one of the hands to saddle a horse for you. Help yourself to any one, although I'd recommend Pixie Dust. She'd got a disposition like an angel." He smiled at Savannah before leaving. "Like you."

Dallas really was very sweet, Savannah thought as she walked to the stables. It was such a shame that he didn't smile more often. A man like that deserved to be happy. She fervently hoped that he would find someone someday to make him as happy as his late wife had.

As she walked, Savannah kept one eye out for Cruz. It wasn't to try to get his attention if she saw him, but to avoid it. She really did want to be alone with her thoughts right now, to try to sort them out.

"Can I help you with anything, *señorita?*" Cruz was just walking out of the stables as she hurried in.

So much for trying to avoid him. "No, I just want to get a horse."

"Choose one, I'll saddle it for you." Cruz gestured into the stable.

Savannah wanted to do it herself. She'd never gotten the knack of being pampered. And she certainly didn't want to be waited on by *him.* "That's all right. I'm sure you're busy. I know how to saddle a horse."

"Why didn't you tell me you were staying on at the ranch?"

Startled, Savannah's hands froze on the saddle horn. She'd just placed the saddle on a strawberry mare and was about to tighten the cinch under the horse's belly. Well, gossip sure did travel fast, she supposed. She tried to look nonchalant as she glanced at Cruz over her shoulder.

"I didn't think you'd be interested." It was an honest answer, if not the *complete* truth.

Nudging her gently aside, Cruz took over tightening the cinch. "I'm interested in everything about you, don't you know that?"

The man could melt steel at thirty paces with that look, Savannah thought. And she wasn't steel.

Savannah shook her head. "It's all right—I relieve you of it."

He looked completely lost. "Of what?"

"Of the need to be charming around me." She tried to look serious, and only partially succeeded. "Cruz, if we're going to keep running into each other like this, you're going to grow very tired of being so devastatingly charming to me."

His eyes slid over her in a look that could only be called possessive. His smile was wide. "Never."

Savannah sighed. "Why don't you just treat me the way you treat Vanessa? It might make it easier on both of us."

Especially on her, she thought. She didn't know just how much longer she could keep resisting him. It was important to stop the game now, before she became too addicted to what he might offer. And too devastated when he didn't offer it any longer.

Picking up the reins, Cruz led the mare out for her. "Well, for one thing, I never made love with Vanessa."

Savannah had never even considered that possibility. Now that Cruz mentioned it, she realized that Vanessa and him making love was something that very well could have happened—growing up on the ranch together and being so close.

But she believed him when he said they hadn't. Words slid effortlessly from his tongue like golden honey pouring from a pitcher, but somehow she believed him. Besides, surely if Vanessa had ever been romantically involved with him, she would have said something when Savannah confessed about being pregnant with Cruz's baby.

Still, Vanessa was one of the most beautiful people, inside and out, that Savannah had ever known. She couldn't understand Cruz not making a play for her friend. "Why didn't you?"

His smile grew a little less lethal. "Because she's like a sister to me."

For some men, that wouldn't have meant much. But Savannah knew what a high regard Cruz had for his family. It hadn't taken long to discover. She could tell by the way she'd seen him kiss his mother on the cheek at the reception, the way he'd looked at his sister Maggie when she'd talked to some of the male guests. There was affection and an air of the protector about Cruz when it came to his family.

All the things, she thought, that had been missing from her own life, her own family. They had been three polite, well-educated people forced to live with one another for a time—all because of one mistake.

The same mistake she'd made, but wasn't going to compound, even though a part of her ached to have Cruz in her life any way she could. Each time she was around him, she found herself more drawn, more attracted. More wistful. And more resolved not to make her parents' misjudgment. Love did not bloom under adversity. Only hostility did.

"I don't know if that makes Vanessa lucky, or not," Savannah commented.

The remark started Cruz wondering about her again. Was she as genuine as she seemed? Or was it all just a very clever act? When he was with her, he could swear that she was completely sweet, completely innocent. Yet away from Savannah, when thoughts had time to ferment and impressions faded, Cruz found himself thinking she had to be like the rest.

Didn't she?

He glanced toward his own horse. Hellfire stood in the corral, jealously watching him work with the other horse. A thought began to form, created by impulse.

"That would be for you to judge," he told her, "not me."

The conversation was headed toward hotter

MARIE FERRARELLA 65

ground than she wanted to tread on. Savannah took
the reins from him.

"If I'm going to be working for the Fortunes,
you and I are going to have to come to some sort
of mutual agreement."

His eyes sparkled. She was playing hard to get,
he realized. Nothing he loved better than a chal-
lenge. It made him want her that much more. The
fact that he'd already had her didn't really enter
into the picture.

His eyes cut the distance between them until
there was nothing. "I'm all for that."

Savannah tried to pull her wits together. Cruz
was making it very hard to think. "We're going to
have to have a *working* arrangement."

Just what he had in mind. He ran his hand up
along her elbow and had the pleasure of seeing a
spark of desire enter her eyes. "You know what
they say. All work and no play..."

She thought of everything Vanessa had told her
after she'd made her confession. Cruz's conquests
were legion. "No one can accuse you of that."

"No," he agreed. "They can't." His brown
eyes darkened a shade. "But I work hard for my
keep. No one can say any less than that, either."

Had she offended him? There was so much pride
in Cruz, so much in the way for her to wade
through. She knew she didn't want to inadvertently

put him down. Even if she never wanted to tell him that the child she carried was his, she still wanted to get to know him. For her baby's sake, as well as her own. To get to know him and to perhaps become his friend, at least for a little while. Her parents had been lovers, but never friends—and in the end, Savannah knew it was friendship that kept love alive.

He held the reins for her as she mounted the horse. "So, where are you going?"

She looked toward the wide, open spaces that beckoned to her. "Just for a ride. To clear my head a little."

He still held on to the reins, even though she reached for them. "Alone?"

Firmly, she leaned over and took the reins from his hand. "I don't mind being alone. Dallas offered to come with me, but—"

At the mention of the other man, she saw Cruz's mouth harden just a fraction.

Dallas again. Was there something serious going on between them? Dallas had his own house on the ranch, yet Cruz knew that last night, the other man had slept in the big house.

As had Savannah.

He raised his chin, his eyes cool. "And you turned him down?"

Why was he looking at her that way? What had

she said? "I didn't want to take him away from anything."

"That's very kind of you." The smile returned, as if nothing at all had crossed his mind except to enjoy the day as it unfolded. "But we can't have you riding around and getting lost. I'll come with you."

She looked toward the corral. It was where Cruz worked to train each horse individually. There was one in there now. "Aren't you working?"

Taking hold of the mare's bit to keep Savannah from suddenly riding off, he led her horse over to his own horse. Releasing Pixie Dust, Cruz easily slid onto Hellfire. He needed no saddle, no reins—just his skill.

"Even employees get to have a lunch break. I'm just taking mine a little early." Cruz gestured for her to lead the way. "I was about to go for a ride anyway."

Savannah turned the mare toward the open country. "Where would you have gone if you hadn't seen me?"

"To a very lonely place. Now it won't be so lonely."

Savannah shook her head. Heaven help her, but she was enjoying this, even when she knew it wasn't real. "You don't stop, do you?"

Cruz was the picture of innocence. "Stop what?"

She played along, though she knew that he knew exactly what she meant. "Flattering."

Solemnly, he shook his head. "Not when I'm inspired by an angel."

If she was an angel, she thought, it was of the fallen variety. "What we did that night wasn't very angelic."

"No?" His brows rose so that they melted into the hair that fell into his eyes. "I could have sworn I heard heavenly music and angels singing at one point." He saw her looking up at the sky as if she was searching for something. Or waiting. "What are you doing?"

"Looking for lightning." An impish smile curved her mouth, though she tried to sound serious. "It should be striking you at any minute."

He laughed, kicking his heels into the horse's flanks to pick up a little speed. "Lightning never strikes down a man who speaks the truth."

Savannah slanted a knowing look in his direction. "Yes, I know."

Cruz laughed again.

Maybe she shouldn't have come.

God knows she'd wanted to. The minute she'd turned around to see Cruz at the stables, she'd wanted to be alone with him like this. But it wouldn't be right, not with this secret between them.

And making love with him, the way she so desperately wanted to do, would only further entangle her heart. She had to concentrate on the future, not the immediate moment, no matter what sort of ecstasy it promised to bring.

But all her logical thoughts kept flying away from her, just as they had that first night they'd been together. Cruz had that kind of effect on her. Just being near her, he drew every scrap of common sense out of her head and replaced it with a yearning so huge that it was almost unmanageable.

They'd been in the meadow now for at least half an hour. Cruz had been nothing but gentlemanly in his advances, touching nothing more intimate than her arm or her neck. He still managed to reduce her to a mass of needs that were better off unsated.

She'd had to fight herself more than she had him.

Stepping away as he came closer to her, Savannah glanced down at her wrist. When she raised her eyes again, she saw that he was looking at her, bemused.

"You keep looking at your watch. If you're expecting someone, they won't be coming here.'' He stared deep into her eyes. "This place is special.''

From up here, with the valley below, she had to admit that the view was spectacular. How many women had he brought here before her? She had to keep that foremost in mind.

"Conjured it up just for me, did you?''

Being out here had always been a humbling experience for Cruz. It put the world, and his ambitions, into perspective. He and his sister Maggie had discovered this place as kids. He came here mostly to be alone with his thoughts. Instinctively, he'd known Savannah would like it. Being here with her seemed right somehow.

"If I could have, I would have. You belong in a place like this. It puts the beauty of nature up against a gauge.''

Savannah rolled her eyes. He really knew how to take the most blatant of lies and make it sound like the truth. Or perhaps she just desperately wanted to believe that he meant at least a small part of what he was saying. And that he cared about her, even a little.

If there was a seedling, it could be nurtured to grow....

Oh, damn, what was she doing, trying to create hope in the middle of a hopeless situation?

She ran the tip of her tongue along her lips. "I

was looking at my watch because I don't want you to be late, getting back.''

Coming up behind her, he slid his hands over her arms. And felt her shiver involuntarily against him. A fire leaped through his veins. Far more demanding than what he'd felt when he thought Dallas had bedded her.

"Let me worry about me," Cruz said softly. His warm breath whispered along the sensitive flesh along her neck.

Savannah could feel her stomach tightening.

"Besides, I don't punch a clock," Cruz told her. "That's not how horse training is done."

Keep him talking. If he talks, he can't kiss. And if he can't kiss, I can't melt.

"How is it done?" Her own voice sounded incredibly squeaky and thin to her ear.

"With skill." She could feel his mouth curving into a smile against her neck. "Just like making love with a woman."

He knew he could have her if he pressed the tiniest bit. But something held him back. So instead of stoking the fire he knew was already burning, Cruz laid his cheek against hers.

"Look out there."

Below their feet, stretching out to eternity, was perhaps the most breathtaking valley she had ever seen. She sighed softly, letting the serenity soothe her. "It's beautiful."

Cruz saw more than just beauty, he saw solitude. A place where a man's place in life didn't matter.

"Nothing for miles." Suddenly, he wanted her with an intensity he'd rarely felt. But he needed her to come to him on her own, not be seduced into doing it. It wouldn't count unless she came to him.

Slowly, he turned her around to face him. "No one would see us. It's far more isolated than a stable."

Her heart lodged itself in her throat, taking up a position that was becoming increasingly familiar. "Did you bring me here just to make love with me?"

His eyes held hers. What was it about her that drew him in like this?

"I would bring you anywhere to make love with you, Savannah. And there is no 'just' about it." He broke with tradition, and told her the truth, if only just this once. "I've had you on my mind ever since that night."

God, how she wished she could believe him.... But she knew she'd just be fooling herself. Men like Cruz Perez didn't remember a single encounter like the one they'd shared. If she were being honest, it surprised her that he even remembered her name. Granted, he hadn't left her abruptly after it was over, with some hurried, flimsy excuse. Instead, he'd held her in his arms, murmuring softly to her in Spanish. She'd been afraid to ask him what the words meant—afraid because they wouldn't be what she'd wanted them to be: a promise.

It was a silly notion, then and now. She knew his reputation. And her own inexperience. The two did not make for a memorable encounter for someone like Cruz.

With effort, she left the shelter of his arms. "I flatter easily, Cruz, but don't mistake that for stupidity."

He looked intrigued. "I would never think of you as stupid, *querida*." Not to be outmaneuvered, Cruz slipped his arms around her waist. It struck him that something had changed since the last time they'd made love. "You feel thinner." He glanced down at her waist. "Are you losing weight?"

Savannah caught her lower lip between her teeth. Right now, thanks to morning sickness she *was* losing weight. But that would all change soon.

Trying to be casual, she shrugged, her arms moving against his. "Nerves."

He studied her face carefully. The revelation further intrigued him. A ploy, or honesty? "What are you nervous about?"

So many things. You. This reckless feeling inside me.

Savannah caught herself before she blurted out more than she intended. Instead, she told him, "New jobs always make me nervous."

"I think it's more than that." He searched her face. Cruz narrowed his eyes. "Do I make you nervous?"

Savannah took a deep breath. Lies were always hard on her. She'd never really managed to tell them with any sort of flair.

"Maybe," she admitted. "Just a little."

The confession caught him off guard. Women were rarely honest with him. He found it a rather charming quality. And very disarming.

Bending, he kissed her cheek instead of her lips. "Then I won't give you anything to be nervous about." This time, he added silently. Cruz looked into her eyes. "We have time."

Rather than quell her nerves, he'd made them jump even more. He was far too close for Savannah to think rationally. The only solution was distance.

"Speaking of which—" She held up her wristwatch for his perusal.

"Yes, I know." Lowering her wrist, he took her

hand in his and began walking back to where they'd tethered the horses. ''Maybe we should be getting back. I've given her enough time to feel secure that I'm not returning to plague her. She'll be surprised to find me nudging at her heels again.''

Savannah wasn't sure whether he was talking about the horse he was training, or about her. In either case, her sympathies were with the mare.

Five

Savannah returned to Dallas the following week to pack up her belongings and bring an end to that chapter of her life. She gave away some of her furniture to charitable organizations and had the rest shipped out to the Double Crown. Dallas had promised to help make room for her things in the suite she now occupied at the ranch.

When her furniture finally arrived, Cruz was the one who insisted on bringing the pieces upstairs for her. Dallas was busy elsewhere.

As they worked to find a suitable arrangement for the furniture, Savannah felt a little as if they were playing house. She tried not to let her imagination get the best of her, but had to admit that it was a nice feeling.

Just the way being with Cruz was.

She saw him often in the time that Vanessa and Devin were away on their honeymoon. And whenever she could, she would watch him work, fascinated by the way he seemed to be able to silently communicate with the magnificent animals he trained. She could see the small corral from the window of the first-floor room where an office had been set up for her. At times, Savannah would pause and stare at man and beast—stare and marvel as Cruz seemed to bond more with the horse with each passing day. It was a thing of beauty to watch as it developed.

There was a whole other side to Cruz that Savannah hadn't realized existed. A gentle, patient, intuitive side. With all her heart, she prayed that more than Cruz's good looks, the baby whose heart beat beneath hers would inherit this special quality.

"Claudia tells me that you and Cruz are seeing a lot of each other."

Engrossed in her work, Savannah didn't register Vanessa's voice until a second after she looked up. Vanessa was standing in the doorway, wearing a smile reminiscent of a cat that had just discovered a secret entrance to an aviary.

"Vanessa!" Pushing her chair back, Savannah hurried to embrace the other woman. "When did you get back?"

"Just now. Claudia waylaid me out front before I even walked in." She stepped back to look at Savannah. "So, is it true?"

Nothing, it seemed, was sacred—or secret—on the Double Crown. After four weeks, Savannah was acutely aware of that. Everyone had been wonderful to her. But everyone, apparently, took an avid interest in everyone else's business. It was one big family, all right—forever intertwined.

Savannah wanted to talk to Vanessa about her honeymoon, not about her own activities. "We've gone riding a few times."

Vanessa looked at her hopefully. "And?"

Savannah shrugged. There was nothing to tell, really. At least, not in the way Vanessa wanted. She and Cruz had enjoyed each other's company, and once or twice been on the cusp of making love, but something had always gotten in the way. Savannah felt both relieved and a little edgy about it.

"And he's been very nice."

"Nice doesn't tell me anything. Oh, Savannah, I want you to be happy—as happy as Devin and me." She smiled the bright, sentimental smile of a new bride. Then she seemed to grow a little more serious. "What about the baby?" She looked at Savannah hopefully. "Does he—?"

Savannah anticipated her question. "No. And he's never going to."

She could see what was going on in Vanessa's mind as clearly as if it were written down on paper. Vanessa was dying to let Cruz know about this baby. But Savannah was adamant about not wanting to trap him. Nothing good could come of her telling him about the baby. If he offered to marry her, she'd have to turn him down. And if he didn't propose, she would be heartbroken that he cared so little. It was best not to bring the matter up at all. Ever.

"Promise?" Savannah pressed.

"Promise," Vanessa echoed, frustrated. "I can keep that part a secret, but we have to face the fact that pretty soon everyone is going to know there's a baby coming."

"A baby?"

Both women jumped at the sound of Cruz's voice. Turning, they stared as he strode into the office. He'd heard that Vanessa was back, but it was Savannah who he'd wanted to see. Walking in on the two women, he'd heard enough to realize that the ranks of the Fortunes were swelling again.

His face was lit with a huge smile. Savannah had never seen him look that way, not even when he was working with the horses. His smile was filled with filial affection. It wasn't sexy, it wasn't unsettling; rather, it was bright and heartfelt.

He had a good heart, she thought. It would just never belong to her.

Cruz went straight to Vanessa, caught her up in his arms and spun her around. He kissed her soundly on the cheek before setting her down again.

"A baby." His grin was wide enough to split his face. "That's wonderful. Congratulations!"

Savannah and Vanessa exchanged looks.

"No, don't worry, I won't tell anyone. I'll keep your secret as long as you want, Vanessa. But I don't see why you'd want to keep it quiet. You've told Devin, haven't you? A man should know when he's about to become a father."

Each word drove a sharp knife through Savannah's heart. Everything, she knew, would change, if he knew that the child he was raving about so joyously was his, and not Devin's.

She looked at Vanessa, but her friend gave no indication that she was going to say anything to correct Cruz. Savannah knew that for the sake of their friendship, Vanessa wouldn't set Cruz straight until she absolutely had to. In the meantime, there would be awkward repercussions. What about Devin? And Vanessa's father? Or Dallas? If this went any further—and it would—they'd all think that Vanessa was pregnant.

No, she wasn't about to put Vanessa through any of that. Not on her account.

Not quite knowing what she was about to say until the words were out, Savannah said, "Vanessa's not the one who's pregnant."

Confusion creased his brow. "But I heard the two of you talking. If she's not pregnant, who is?"

Savannah swallowed. The admission came out in a whisper. "I am."

The smile abruptly vanished from Cruz's face as he looked at her in stunned silence.

In a heartbeat, tension became a fourth entity in the room.

Vanessa looked from Savannah to Cruz. "Maybe I should go."

Savannah didn't want to be alone with Cruz. Not until she could think clearly and come up with something believable to answer the questions she dreaded were coming. Her eyes darted toward Vanessa. "No, that's all right, there's nothing going on here that you can't stay for." Savannah was surprised that she could even form words when her mouth felt so dry and her pulse was racing so fast that she actually heard it vibrating in her ears.

Cruz's eyes never left Savannah's face, his expression too dark to read. "Yes, thank you, Vanessa. If you don't mind, I would like to speak to Savannah alone."

Torn, Vanessa hesitated, not knowing who to accommodate. She was closer to Savannah, but she'd known Cruz all of her life.

Savannah inclined her head, silently telling Vanessa that it was all right to go.

"I'll be close by," she whispered to Savannah before closing the door behind her.

The silence in the room was deafening. Tension grew another two feet in height and width.

A thousand words rushed into Savannah's head, and flew out again just as quickly. Unable to think clearly, she held her tongue and waited for Cruz to say something to her—praying that she wouldn't lose her courage and blurt out the truth if he asked for it. There would be no winners then, only three losers.

Cruz circled around her slowly, like a man searching for the hidden entrance to a sealed citadel. "You're pregnant."

Hands clenched at her sides, Savannah refused to turn and look at him as he moved around her. "Yes."

How long had she known? Did she know she was pregnant when she rode with him to the meadow? Or danced so closely with him at the reception? Or smiled so invitingly at him these past weeks? Was everything just an act?

Or—?

His eyes narrowed. "You're sure?"

Savannah steeled herself. "Yes."

He was standing in front of her again, his eyes on hers. Looking for signs, for lies. For the truth. "Is it mine?"

Yes!

The word screamed inside her brain. Savannah

could feel it vibrating within her body, begging for release. But she was still determined not to compound her mistake by making another, more grievous one. She had to make the best of a bad situation.

The best meant never making the child feel the brunt of the guilt—even if the words were never spoken—for having forced its parents together. The way she had unwittingly forced her own parents together. A sense of guilt had pervaded her entire childhood as a result. It was no way to raise a child, no way to seal together a family. And she wasn't about to commit that sin, no matter what she felt for Cruz.

Because all he would feel, eventually, would be resentment toward her.

She looked directly into his eyes, praying that he would forgive her for lying if he ever found out. "No, the baby isn't yours."

Relief flowed over him. But it immediately dried up in the heat of the surprising anger that followed. Anger that flamed high, hiding the hurt that hovered just behind it.

If it wasn't his, then whose? Dallas's? No, it was too soon for the baby to belong to Dallas. But maybe not. Maybe Savannah and Dallas had been together before. If they had, then what did that make him? Intermission?

Something bitter twisted deep within Cruz.

"Is Dallas the father?"

Surprise at his question gave way to hurt. Was that what he thought of her? That she slept around? Well, she reasoned, what *could* he think, if she'd just told him that the baby wasn't his?

Logic did little to assuage the hurt she felt. Her thoughts were too painful. Unable to deal with them now, she blocked them out.

"Why are you cross-examining me?"

It wasn't easy keeping his temper in check, not when he wanted to shake the answer out of her. "Is he?" Cruz demanded, his voice hardly above a hoarse, barely restrained whisper.

There was a darkness in his eyes that made her catch her breath. Savannah squared her shoulders, rallying. She could deal with anger far better than she could with kindness or sympathy. Anger begat anger. She clung to that.

"No, if it's any business of yours. Dallas and I are just old friends."

She was lying about some part of this. She had to be. "If the baby isn't mine and it isn't his—"

She didn't want to go any further into the lie than she already had, but clearly he wasn't going to be satisfied with evasions. Cruz wanted an answer, and she knew he wouldn't leave her alone until she gave him one. She thought of Reese. Naming him would hurt no one.

"If you must know, the baby's father is my fiancé—my ex-fiancé," she clarified when surprise leaped into his eyes.

"Your ex-fiancé," he echoed.

The words made Cruz feel oddly numb. So much so that he wasn't sure just what he *was* feeling. What he should have been feeling at this point was overwhelming relief, not this all-pervading discontent. He remembered how sad her eyes had looked at the christening. He'd prodded her until she'd told him about the broken engagement. Cruz couldn't see her going back to the man.

"The one you told me you were trying to get over?"

"Yes."

Savannah could feel his eyes boring into her. She wanted to look away, but she knew if she did, he'd know she was lying. So she endured the look of censure she saw and burrowed further into the deception.

"We decided to give reconciliation one last try." Savannah shrugged, all the while hating what she was saying. "It didn't take."

His eyes regarded her coldly. She'd burned hot beneath him, then gone running back to a man who had used her so badly. How could she have done that?

"Maybe 'it' didn't, but something obviously did."

Savannah's face remained impassive at the cynical remark, giving Cruz no clue just how much it hurt. She drew herself up.

"The bottom line is that you don't have to worry, Cruz. I won't be coming to you asking for anything."

He was off the hook totally. Every single man's nightmare, and it was over, just like that. Why couldn't he feel better about this than he did? Why couldn't he successfully curtail his anger at finding out that she'd slept with someone else?

"So, will you be going back to *him* asking for anything?"

She didn't like the tone of the question—and certainly not the implication that she would use the baby as a tool to get money.

Her eyes hardened, drawing a curtain over her vulnerability. "It wasn't a planned pregnancy. Possession is nine points of the law. The way I see it, I have possession of the baby, that means the baby is my responsibility and no one else's."

For a second, Cruz's temper cooled a little. He thought of Maggie. His sister had found herself in the same situation when she was pregnant with

Travis. Her husband had shunned his duty completely, choosing instead to divorce her and disappear from her life. And the life of his son.

Cruz remembered how he had felt at the time. Like he wanted to kill her husband with his bare hands. "Fathers have some responsibilities, too."

Responsibilities, but not love, she thought. And love was all she wanted for her baby. And for herself.

"Sometimes, it's best for everyone to leave all that untapped." With effort, Savannah sat down again behind her desk and pretended to shut him out. "Now, if there's nothing else, I have work to do."

"No," he said, barely containing the flash of temper he felt. "There's nothing else."

He slammed the door behind him when he walked out.

Savannah wilted in her chair. She jerked, her eyes darting toward the door when it opened again less than a minute later.

Crossing to her, Vanessa put her arms comfortingly around Savannah. "Are you all right?"

Savannah took a deep breath, then let it out slowly before answering. "No," she admitted. "But I will be."

The way she saw it, she had no other choice.

Six

The lariat slipped out of his hands—that made three times since he'd started today. Muttering a curse, Cruz stooped down and picked it up off the ground. Pickett whinnied, and it sounded suspiciously like a laugh. Cruz's foul mood intensified.

What the hell was the matter with him lately?

He knew the answer to that even as he made the silent demand. Knew the answer, even though it still didn't make any more sense to him now than it had a week ago.

The woman was pregnant and out of his hair. He usually liked it when loose ends took care of themselves, and there was no question that these had. God knew he'd never been one for long-term romances. To him, long term meant maybe a week, if that much. It certainly didn't mean harboring any sort of feelings for a woman for months.

It had been a little more than four months since he'd first slept with Savannah.

And last slept with Savannah.

Disgusted with himself for dwelling on her, and

with Savannah for preying on his thoughts this way, Cruz recoiled the lariat.

But his mind refused to clear.

Right from the beginning, she'd been different. He'd never had a woman linger on his mind, never had an insatiable craving for a woman he'd already had once. And he certainly had never refrained from seducing one if he'd been so inclined and had the opportunity.

Whenever he'd been with Savannah since she'd arrived at the ranch, he'd sensed that all he had to do was push the right buttons—the way he had that first night—and she would be his for the taking. But because she'd tried to resist, he hadn't pushed.

What had he been thinking?

And what was he thinking now?

Instead of using the lariat, he hung it from one of the posts on the small, circular corral. Damn it, it had been almost a week since Savannah had dropped that little bombshell of hers on him, and he was still letting it fester, like a wound he somehow couldn't make himself clean. A wound that hurt every time he touched it.

Ruben frowned as he watched his son working with the horse. Or not working. He'd always been proud of the boy. From the time Cruz was five years old, it was obvious that he had an affinity for animals—horses in particular. More than just an affinity: a gift. He could make horses do anything he set his mind to. A little like the women who were always seeking him out, giving him no peace. Not that Cruz ever seemed to want any.

He'd also shown an early talent for making the most of the opportunities, and the women, who came his way.

But something was wrong. And it had been for more than a week now. Cruz seemed preoccupied, not at ease with himself or the horse he was training. Usually, it was a pleasure to watch him. But for the last week, it had been nothing short of painful.

Rosita had her own theories as to what was bothering their son. She'd sent Ruben here today to check it out. As if he needed an entreaty from his wife to see what was wrong with his son.

Hooking his arms around the top railing, Ruben hoisted himself up for a better view. The horse was roaming about the corral, waiting for Cruz to make a move. But Cruz was just standing still, lost in thought.

"It isn't going well, is it?"

Cruz turned around at his father's question and forced himself to wipe the scowl from his brow. Normally, he didn't mind being watched, but today the results he was after weren't materializing. He didn't like looking like a fool, even to his own family.

His broad shoulders moved up and then down carelessly. "Some horses are slower than others."

"The same could be said of some women." Ruben smiled. "Some take more patience. Those are the ones that are worth waiting for."

Cruz studied his father's sun-bronzed face. "Did you come here to lecture me about women or horses?"

Ruben's eyes were solemn. "I didn't come here to lecture you about anything. You seem restless. Your mother worries."

And so did his father, Cruz thought. But he couldn't help that. He couldn't live his life for others; he had to find his own way. He'd always thought that the path was straightforward. Ever since he was ten, he'd known exactly what he wanted.

And yet...

Cruz stared off toward the horizon. Things had been much clearer before Savannah had come here. "Yes, I'm restless. I'm tired of working for someone else. I want something of my own."

Ruben patted Cruz's thigh in sympathy. "Patience, Cruz."

Cruz felt he'd already been patient far too long,

and it had gotten him nowhere. "Patient people grow old."

Ruben knew what it felt like to be young, to want things immediately. "Patient people *live* to grow old." He thought of his life with Rosita. "Half the pleasure of victory is the path that it took to get there."

"I've been on the same path for a long time— scrimping, saving every dollar. And somehow, it just never seems to be enough. Just a little more, a little more. I want a piece of land—nothing huge—just something my own to start out with. Something to leave my mark on. I want a ranch of my own before I'm too old to sit on a horse."

"I'm more than twenty-five years older than you," replied Ruben. "I can still sit on a horse, still keep up with the likes of you. And my father rode until he was almost eighty."

Focused on his frustration, Cruz didn't hear the encouragement in his father's words. He only gleaned what he wanted to. "That's probably how old I'll be before I can put together enough money to buy a ranch. Seventy-nine, like Grandpa." It was the age at which his grandfather had died.

For a moment, Ruben said nothing. But he knew it wasn't ambition that was making his son so short-tempered today. The drive that burned in

Cruz's chest so brightly was nothing new—the flame had been there for a long time now.

No, it was something else. Something, he had a feeling, that Cruz was not accustomed to dealing with.

Ruben leaned back, looking toward the ranch house. Maybe Rosita was right, after all. "I hear the new woman on the ranch is with child."

Ruben watched in fascination as Cruz's jaw tightened. "Word gets around fast."

"Is it yours?" Even as he asked, he felt he had his answer. That would go a long way toward explaining why his son was acting the way he was. Silently, Ruben tipped his hat to his wife's intuition.

Cruz shot him a look. The question drew fresh irritation. "No."

Children did not always tell their parents the truth, Ruben thought. He hadn't always himself. But there was more than the truth involved here. There was a child's welfare. "A man should never deny his own child."

"I said no!" Cruz snapped. "She told me it wasn't mine. That the baby belongs to some man she was in love with before she came here." The words tasted bitter in his mouth. Why couldn't he make peace with that? Why couldn't he just believe her, and move on?

"But you've been with her."

Resentment flashed in Cruz's eyes, put there by his own confusion. "Since when did you start keeping a diary on me?"

Ruben's face grew stern. His temper was slow, but it could burn just as strongly as Cruz's, once it was stoked. "I would watch my mouth if I were you. You're not too big for me to take a strap to."

"Big words from a man who never raised a hand to any of his children." But Cruz's voice had softened a little. He hadn't meant to be disrespectful. His father didn't deserve being on the receiving end of his temper.

"One is never too old to learn." Ruben looked at him pointedly. "Never."

Taking off his hat, Cruz dragged a hand through his hair. For a long moment, he watched the horse move about the small enclosure, anxious to be free. Like him. Savannah was releasing him of all responsibility, telling him the child wasn't his. Why wasn't he content with that?

He flashed an apologetic grin at his father. "You're right. I'm sorry. And yes, I've been with her. But that doesn't matter."

"Perhaps it does."

Wearily, Cruz put his hat back on. "What are you getting at?"

Ruben smiled. "Only that maybe she wasn't telling the truth."

Cruz looked at his father. "You think she lied about the baby?"

"About who the father is, perhaps."

It didn't make any sense to Cruz. Savannah would have everything to gain by telling him. "Why?"

"I don't know." Ruben shrugged. "Perhaps because she does not want you to feel responsible. Perhaps she does not want to be a burden." He paused. "Perhaps she does not think you would be a good father. Or perhaps she has heard about your plans to be your own man, to own your own place, and she knows that a child would rob you of those dreams, at least for a little while." He looked at Cruz. "Does she know about your dreams?"

Cruz crossed back to where he had left the lariat. It was time to get back to work, back to what he knew and understood. For all his experience with women, he didn't understand them. All he understood was how to make them feel good, and how to live in the moment.

But his time with Savannah had been different. They *had* done more than enjoy each other. He and Savannah had talked a great deal. She had been a good audience, and he had caught himself sharing feelings with her more than once—something he'd never before done with a woman he'd slept with.

Turning around again, he shrugged in reply. "I might have mentioned them."

"Did she listen?"

"Yes, she listened." And that had been what had intrigued him about her. Savannah hadn't just pretended to listen. She really had listened.

"Then perhaps you have your answer. Perhaps she does not want to rob you of those dreams of yours."

Irritation, not far from the surface these last few days, leaped up. "Why are you so convinced that this is my baby?"

His father's gaze was unwavering. "Why are you so convinced that it isn't?"

"Because she…told me." Begun with conviction, the sentence dribbled away into doubt. Cruz saw the look on his father's face and realized the error of his logic.

Ruben laid a hand on his son's shoulder. The support was silent, but strong, nonetheless, and understood. "My point is made. If I were you, I would ask her again. And then a third time, as well. The truth will come out if you look for it hard enough."

Maybe it was better to leave well enough alone. Maybe he really didn't want the truth. And maybe,

Cruz thought in annoyance, he no longer knew what he wanted. "If it is my child—"

Ruben spoke to him, not father to son, but man to man. "Then you have a right to know."

He felt like a dog chasing his own tail. "But if she doesn't want me to know, then there isn't anything I can do about it. I can't force the answer out of her. Savannah even said it was for the best if the baby's father wasn't told."

"And you need more proof than that?"

Cruz shook his head. His father didn't understand. "She was talking about this college man of hers, this man she was to marry before he broke it off."

"And you felt she was telling the truth?"

Savannah was right. It was best just to leave this whole thing alone. Better for him, and maybe, for reasons he didn't quite understand, better for her, as well.

Taking the lariat, he threw the loop over the stallion's head again. The horse didn't flinch this time.

"As you pointed out, Dad, I have dreams. I'm not going to go buying trouble."

Ruben laughed softly as he got down from the railing. "Perhaps you have already made a down payment on it." He thought of the years that had gone into forming the man who stood before him now. Years Ruben never once regretted spending.

"Besides, I have never thought of a child as trouble."

Cruz appreciated what was being said, appreciated the love and guidance he'd received over the years. But he knew his limitations. "I'm not you, Dad."

"No," Ruben agreed, "you are not." They were different, he and Cruz, in so many ways. But in others, in matters that counted, they were the same. He knew that even if Cruz didn't yet. "But you are an honorable man, same as me, even if you try to behave like some wild, untamable mustang. You cannot hide from your true nature forever."

With that, Ruben turned away from the corral and walked away.

Cruz looked after him thoughtfully. He felt the horse nudge him from behind and then laughed. "All right, I know you like attention and I've ignored you long enough. Let's get to work."

Cruz did what made him happiest, and purged his mind of all other thoughts.

Seven

Dallas shook his head in amazement as he looked over the neatly bound report that Savannah had just handed him. Though he'd said words to the contrary, part of him had felt that perhaps Savannah had been given the bookkeeping job out of sympathy. Now he realized just how fortunate they were to have her working for them.

The woman gave a hundred fifty percent in every capacity, anticipating requests before they were even made, compiling statistics still warm from being formed. In six short weeks, she had gone from bookkeeper to treasure.

Setting the report down on her desk, he grinned broadly at her. "Savannah, I don't know what we ever did without you."

Savannah smiled and placed the report into the "to file" stack. "Relied on your other bookkeeper would be my guess."

That's what he liked about her. The fact that she didn't have so much as a hint of an inflated ego. The woman was as unassuming as they came.

As he picked up his hat, he glanced at his watch. He had a plane to catch in less than two hours, and there was still the trip to the airport to face. But he lingered a moment, determined to exchange a few words with Savannah. In the ever-hurried pace that surrounded the ranch, there never seemed to be enough time for amenities.

"Nathan was never as efficient as you, Savannah. Thank God, Vanessa had the presence of mind to offer you the position when she did."

Savannah thought of how the job had been a godsend to her; it had put an end to the soul-wearying task of trying to find a job, while debating just what to say about her "condition." This might be the tail end of the nineties, but some things resisted change. Such as an employer's desire not to waste money on a woman who might not return to her position once her baby was born.

She was the one who was grateful to them for helping her out of her dilemma, at least the financial end of it. "Thank you."

Their eyes met, and work and plane schedules were tabled for the moment. "Is there anything I can do for you, Savannah?"

No, there wasn't anything he could do—any more than he'd already done. The kind tone almost made her cry. Savannah shook her head as she picked up a stack of reports.

"Just throw in a compliment like that every now and then, and I'll be fine."

"No problem." He followed her to the file cabinet. "I'll be in Europe for about four weeks, but if there's anything you need to reach me about, here's the number of my hotel. I don't want Dad dealing with any more than he already has to." Dallas frowned, his features darkening slightly. "He's got enough on his hands trying to extricate himself from the wicked witch of the west's clutches."

No one, Savannah had quickly discovered, liked Sophia Fortune. She hadn't met the woman herself, but from all reports, Ryan's soon-to-be ex-wife was selfish, self-centered and despicable. It was a wonder that the woman had pulled the blinders over Ryan's eyes long enough to get him to marry her. But he'd been vulnerable right after his first wife Janine had died, and Sophia had apparently used that to her advantage.

A lot of wrong moves could be chalked up to vulnerability, Savannah thought. She closed her fingers over the paper with the hotel number.

Dallas picked up the travel bag he'd thrown together. "Then I'll see you when I get back." Turning, he almost ran into Cruz on his way out. "Sorry—didn't see you standing there. Want to see me about something? I'm in a hurry, Cruz."

Cruz shook his head, his easy smile betraying none of the emotions simmering beneath. "No, I just came to see Savannah."

Dallas's mouth curved. "Then I'll get out of your way." The next moment, he was gone.

Damn, when was she going to be able to look at Cruz without feeling her heart leap into her throat?

Nerve endings rose, stiffening like tiny hairs in a breeze. Savannah didn't know where to look, what to do with herself. She hadn't been alone with him for almost two weeks—ever since she'd told him that she was pregnant.

But because of her office's orientation, she found herself watching Cruz work with his horse far more than she should. Watching, and letting her mind drift to a world that was perfect. A world where resentment and repercussions didn't exist. And love did.

Forcing a smile to her lips, she looked at him. "What can I do for you?"

You can tell me the truth.

His smile remained, sensual and teasing, as he shoved his hands into his back pockets. She looked a little pale, he thought. He wondered if that was because of the baby, or because she never seemed to go outside. At least, he hadn't seen her around lately.

"Just stopped by to see how you were doing." He took a deep breath. The room smelled of wood and lemon polish—his mother's handiwork. But the scent of exotic flowers was new. Savannah's. "It's been about two weeks since I've seen you."

Two weeks in which he'd tried to blot Savannah out of his system. It might have worked, too, if he didn't have dreams that insisted on sneaking up on him in the middle of the night. Dreams about limbs as soft as cream, eyes as blue as the sky, and a smile made out of sunshine.

She came to him like that—a misty, unattainable dream—making him yearn for her. Making him doubt his own sanity when he awoke.

With the studied air of a man whose most serious thought was of his latest conquest, Cruz sat down on the edge of the desk and looked down at her. His eyes swept over her with familiar ease.

"So, tell me, how's it going?" Her figure was as shapely as ever; there wasn't so much as a hint of the baby that was to come.

She raised her eyes to his. "Professionally or personally?"

"Whatever you want to tell me."

She pretended that she was still talking to Dallas. It was easier for her that way.

"I miss teaching, but the work is interesting and everyone's been very kind." She looked around at the stacks of files that were still piled up on the desk. "I never realized that there was so much involved in running a ranch."

He knew about that end all too well. It wasn't just about the horses. Unbeknownst to his family, he'd taken several correspondence courses in management to learn that end of it. He meant to have his own ranch—not just dream about it.

But the ranch was the furthest thing from his mind right now. It took a great deal of effort not to reach out and touch her; he was so close.

With renewed determination, he kept his hands still. "And personally?"

Savannah would have looked away if she were able. Instead, her eyes were held prisoner by the look she saw in his.

"Like I said, everyone's been very nice."

The sensual smile melted into a genuine one. "You're an easy person to be nice to. What do you do when you're not working?"

She said the first thing that came into her head. "Read." Savannah had gathered together an armload of baby books and books on parenting. She felt hopelessly unprepared for the coming event, but was trying to get a handle on it.

"I was wondering if maybe you'd like to go for a ride later." He heard himself fumbling. He hadn't fumbled around a woman since he was fifteen. He didn't know whether to be amused, or sincerely worried, about the implications. "If there's no problem?"

Her brows furrowed in confusion. "Problem?"

His eyes lowered to her flat belly. "I mean in your condition..."

Cruz didn't know how to put it. He hated this awkward feeling. Part of him wasn't even sure what he was doing here. He only knew that he missed seeing her. Who knew? Maybe she even needed a friend. He could do that much for her.

Hell, he wanted more than that and he knew it. But it was a start.

"It'll be a peaceful ride in the country, not the first lap of the Kentucky Derby. I think I can safely manage it without worrying about my 'condition.'"

Cruz nodded, pleased at the answer. Maybe too pleased, but he'd deal with that later, he told himself. "When's the baby due, anyway?"

"The beginning of March."

Absorbing the information, Cruz rose. "All right, so I'll see you about five. Will that be all right?"

She was free to make her own hours, Dallas had been very liberal about that. But she wasn't sure about Cruz's time table. "Is that when you get off? Five?"

The idea of regular, restricting hours had always rankled him. That was why he could have never left to hold down a job like his sisters. Confinement, any sort of confinement, visible or otherwise, wasn't for him. He had to be free.

"I told you, it's not like punching a clock. I put in a certain amount of time to train a horse. How I do it depends on me—and the horse."

"Then make it for three o'clock."

With a wink, he inclined his head. "Three it is."

For the first time in two weeks, as she got back to her work a few minutes later, Savannah really felt like smiling.

The beginning of March.

The words hummed through Cruz's mind. He had made love with her at Bryan's christening. The beginning of June. That left the count at nine months.

He'd bet his soul that the baby wasn't a consequence of any aborted, short-lived reconciliation between Savannah and her ex-fiancé. The baby she was carrying was his, plain and simple.

Despite the jealousy he'd felt when he'd seen Dallas dancing with Savannah and paying attention to her, Cruz knew in his heart that Savannah wasn't the kind of woman who slept around. He needed no affidavits, no sworn statements to sway him one way or another. Some things a man just knew.

Which made the responsibility he was grappling with all the more difficult.

On the one hand were his dreams—dreams that required hard work and the kind of sacrifice he had no right to ask anyone else to make for him. The kind of sacrifice that would test his own metal.

On the other was a wide-eyed, gentle woman who, for reasons he didn't understand, refused to use what was at her disposal to ensnare him. Many of the women he had bedded had been manipulating and self-absorbed. But not Savannah.

Unless... Was she such a grand master at deception that she had him completely fooled? Completely blinded to the truth?

His mouth curved in a mocking smile as he stopped at the corral. Somehow, he doubted it, but he'd walked too long on a cynical path to be completely divorced from the possibility.

At the very least, he'd suspend making a decision until he knew just what, if anything, she was up to. Climbing over the railing, he jumped down into the corral, picking up his lariat where he'd left it. The horse, a new stallion he'd been working with since only the day before yesterday, eyed him like an adversary.

That would change soon, Cruz silently promised

the animal. Easily, with soft words of assurance, he approached the skittish quarter horse.

Cruz had to admit that for reasons that weren't entirely clear to him, he wanted Savannah to own up to the baby's parentage. It wasn't because he had a crying need to pass on his genes and his name to another, or to see himself immortalized in the small features of a child's face. That had never been even a remote desire. If he thought of children at all, he thought of them as belonging to other people.

True, he loved his sisters' children. His nieces and nephews always generated a warm feeling within him, but they were family, and feeling that way was safe. They were not his to provide for, only his to spoil. He had the best of all worlds, and he meant to keep it that way.

He meant to reach his goals and not end up like his father: a man who took off his hat to someone else, who obeyed someone else and came home at the end of each day to a small house on someone else's land.

The horse stood still, watching his every move. He advanced slowly, gaining ground. Gaining the animal's confidence.

Savannah wasn't going to trap him, Cruz thought.

But she isn't trying, a small voice reminded him.

If anything, he had been the one to seek her out, not the other way around. She'd done nothing to place herself in his path.

Nothing—but prey on his mind.

It was enough.

"There," he murmured to the horse, running his hands along the animal's silken muzzle. "That wasn't so bad, was it?"

As he slipped the lariat around the animal's neck, the question echoed in his head, replaying itself over and over again.

Fall was in the air, crisp and fresh, accompanied by a wind that was a little less than gentle, a little more than soft. It whipped through Savannah's hair in sudden spurts of energy before settling down again to an even rhythm, and running long, stroking fingers through the tall grass.

It was brisk, and Cruz half expected Savannah to turn her horse around a few minutes into the ride and suggest that they return to the ranch. But she'd surprised him by urging her horse on into a canter, her face radiant. Her laughter blended with the sound of the wind, equally intriguing to him.

She seemed one with the elements, yet so much above them that she made him ache just to see her.

She made him ache, just being near.

They finally stopped by a stream, dismounting

to let the horses rest and graze. He watched as Savannah turned her face up to the sky. She closed her eyes, still glowing, as if she wanted the breeze to caress her. As if she were soaking up everything that the day had to offer.

He'd never known another woman quite like her.

The wind teased her hair into her face. Very gently, Cruz pushed it away before she could. He knew he should move back to give her space, but he couldn't do it. "If it's too windy for you, we can go back."

"Oh, no, this is perfect." She stepped back, spreading her arms as if she were about to embrace everything around her. "I love it like this. It makes you feel glad to be alive."

Bemusement filtered in. She made him think of a little girl playing hooky. "Why?"

The question caught her off guard. It was just a feeling; she hadn't bothered to explore it. Savannah shrugged, laughing as she spun about in a circle. When she swayed a little, he was quick to lock his arms around her, as if he was afraid she was going to fall down.

But she'd done all the falling she intended to.

Very gently, she disengaged herself and moved away.

"I don't know, it just does. It's a rush." She

took a deep breath. "Smell it—the air's sweet and clean and wonderful. It makes me remember when I was a little girl." A flood of memories crowded her mind. Picnics with the grandmother who doted on her. State fairs and long rides in the country on a horse named Strawberry, in the company of a groom who frowned too much and worried that she would fall.

The radiant look on her face made Cruz envious. What was it like, to feel like that? To harbor a ray of happiness so closely that it shone out of every pore?

"What were you like as a little girl?"

She picked up a daisy, almost withered now that autumn had planted itself, and began picking at the petals one by one.

"All knees and elbows." She could step outside of herself and see the little girl she'd been. "I was very skinny and very tall for my age."

"I find that hard to believe."

She laughed, tossing away the stem. "So did my parents. Neither one of them could understand how they could have created between them such a homely child. They were both very beautiful people," she said almost wistfully. When she was little, she would have given anything to look sleek and sophisticated like her mother. Savannah pressed her lips together. "My father suspected that my mother had lied to him."

"Lied?"

"That she'd lied when she told him that she was pregnant with his child." Savannah really wasn't sure why she was sharing this with him. The words just seemed to be coming on their own. "They weren't married at the time. But they were when I was born." Unwilling to see the look in his eyes, Savannah turned her face forward. The day didn't seem quite as pretty as it had been a moment before. "Biggest mistake they ever made."

He was silent as he considered the import of what she'd just said. "Is that why you won't admit the baby's mine?"

Regret was instant. She knew she shouldn't have said anything. "I won't admit the baby's yours because it isn't. I told you—"

He knew what Savannah had told him. Knew too, in his heart, that it was a lie. He didn't need his mother prodding at him the way she'd done over the past few days, telling him to take charge of his responsibility. Telling him that she "felt" the baby was her grandchild.

"I don't have a fancy college degree, but I can do the math, Savannah. If you're due at the beginning of March, the baby was conceived at the beginning of June. When you slept with *me*."

She raised her chin, a bittersweet smile twisting her lips. "As I remember, sleeping wasn't part of it."

"No, it wasn't." Cruz placed his hands on her shoulders so that she couldn't turn away from him again. "Don't try to distract me, Savannah. You're very good at distracting a man." So good that even now it was hard for him to hold himself in check, to keep from taking her into his arms and losing himself in the taste of her lips. "You made love with me at the beginning of June."

She knew she was going to pay dearly for this. Still, she forced the words out of her mouth. "How do you know you were the only one I made love with in June?"

His pride reared at the implication, but he left the bait where it was cast. It was a ruse, a ploy.

"Because I know." His eyes held hers. "I *know* you." Time had nothing to do with that kind of knowledge; it came when one soul understood another. "You told me then that you and your boyfriend had broken up. That he had changed his mind about wanting to get married. A woman doesn't make that kind of admission unless its true."

She pulled away. If he continued holding her, touching her, she was going to weaken. "Women say all kinds of things."

"Maybe they do," he allowed. "But you don't."

Confused, weary, her temper flashed. She was trying to do the right thing. Why wouldn't he let her? "And since when have you become such an expert on me?"

"I don't know. It's just something that happened." Cruz took a deep breath. His father was right. Confronted with the situation, there was only one honorable thing to do. "Marry me, Savannah."

For one thrilling second, the word *yes* hovered in her mind. But then she squelched it. She wouldn't say yes to something that he would live to regret and that she would live to hurt over. He didn't even want to do it now. She saw the reluctance in his eyes, the resignation. How long before that resignation turned to resentment?

"No."

"It's my baby."

Savannah whirled around on her heel, her patience shredding.

"Yes," she shouted, tired of the pretense. "It's your baby. Satisfied?" Before he could answer, she continued. "But you don't have to do anything to atone for it. Can't you understand? I don't *want* anything from you. I don't want your money, your name, your dreams, nothing!" How could she make it any clearer to him than that? "This is *my* baby and *I* will raise him or her. *I* will be the one to take care of him or her, not you." She waved an impatient hand in dismissal. "You're free to go on with your life. I'm giving you your freedom."

"And if I don't want it?" he challenged, his voice rising dangerously.

Who did he think he was fooling? She fisted her hands on her hips. "Every fiber of your being wants it, Cruz. Maybe you do know me, but I know you better. You're the wind, Cruz. Your destiny is to rustle leaves, to go from place to place, leaving your mark, but always moving on. I didn't plan on this, but it happened, and I will deal with it. I don't want to deal with an angry husband, as well. And that's what you'll be. Angry and resentful. I can't face the rest of my life knowing that I'll see that in your eyes."

Doggedly determined to do the right thing, he told her, "You won't."

But she shook her head. Not even the smallest part of her believed the promise. No one could be that blindly optimistic.

"You're not that good an actor. You might even mean it now, but you won't later and later is all there is. An eternity of laters." She crossed back to where the horses were tethered. "So spare me any noble gestures. You don't have to soothe your conscience." Picking up the reins, she faced him. "I'm an independent woman, Cruz. I run up a bill, I pay it. I don't borrow money, or give it to someone else to take care of."

God, but this hurt, she thought. Because she knew, given a chance, that she could be happy with him. Make a life with him.

Savannah looked out on the range. The sky was growing darker. How fitting.

"Maybe you're right. Maybe it is getting too cold to go on riding. I'm going back."

Before he could stop her, she'd swung into the saddle. A second later, the horse was galloping back toward the ranch. And away from him.

Swallowing a ripe curse, Cruz swung into his own hand-tooled saddle and rode after her. He didn't bother calling out because he knew she wouldn't stop.

It was several minutes before he caught up to her. When he was close enough, he whistled, and the horse came to an abrupt stop.

Annoyed, she swung around in her saddle to look at him as he approached. "Very funny."

"Handy," was all he said before his eyes clouded again, growing more ominous than the sky above. "Damn it, woman, what do you think you're doing?"

"Being my own person," she snapped. Savannah pulled the reins out of his hands and kicked her heels into the horse's flanks again.

This time, Cruz let her go.

Eight

"You and I need to talk."

Savannah hadn't expected Cruz to be in her doorway when she'd said, "Come in," in response to the knock. She had been avoiding Cruz for days now, ever since the ride in the meadow.

The book she'd been reading fell from her fingers, slipping to the floor. Ignoring it, she rose to her feet. Sitting made her feel too vulnerable.

Everything about him made her feel vulnerable.

"I really don't think we have anything to talk about," she said stiffly.

"Oh, really?" His eyes were unfathomable as he walked into the room. "And the baby doesn't count?"

She watched him close the door behind him, and gathered her courage. "The baby counts. The baby means everything to me."

Purposefully, she crossed to the door and began to open it again. She didn't want to be alone in the room with him. Her resolve was only so strong; her resistance to him was already weakening.

Cruz caught her wrist in his hand, keeping her from opening the door. "And what about me?"

Her eyes challenged him. "What about you?"

"You don't think the baby means anything to me?"

With a yank, she pulled her wrist free. "The baby will mean a whole lot more to you if you don't have to break your back providing for it."

So what she was saying to him was that she thought he couldn't provide for the baby in the same fashion that someone else could. That he'd have to break his back to do it, to keep the baby in clothes and its belly filled. And she obviously wanted better than that.

She was like the others who populated her world after all.

He stared at her for what felt like a long time, trying to control his feelings, and the flash of temper that had suddenly risen.

Because he didn't trust himself right now, Cruz withdrew without a word.

Savannah was shaken. She stared after him. He'd left, just as she'd wanted him to.

So why wasn't she pleased?

A deep-rooted sadness that she had no idea how to contain filled her. Moving very slowly, like someone walking at the bottom of a pool, she crossed over to the switch and turned off the lights.

Savannah laid down on her bed in the dark, drawing herself together as tightly as she could. And then she began to cry.

It was late. The sun had already risen and set up house within her room, probing at all the corners until it filled everything.

Resisting the sadness she knew was waiting for her, Savannah woke up reluctantly. There was a knot in her belly, far larger than the baby she was carrying.

Her face felt tight and drawn. Sleep had not come for a long time last night. When it had, it was ushered in with tears that refused to subside. Exhaustion had finally overtaken her.

She felt more dead than alive.

Her stomach made its presence known a few seconds after she'd opened her eyes.

"Oh, God, baby," she pleaded in a whisper, "give me a break."

But apparently, she wasn't going to receive a break on any front any time soon. Her hands over her mouth, Savannah bolted and ran for the bathroom.

Twenty minutes later, showered and dressed, Savannah left her room, not necessarily prepared to meet the world, but resigned to it. She got as far as closing her door behind her before running into

Maggie. Literally. Not paying attention, preoccupied with her own thoughts, she collided with Cruz's sister.

"Oh, excuse me. I didn't mean to—" Maggie abruptly halted her apology. "Are you all right?"

Savannah didn't want to be rude, but she was in no mood to talk. "Yes."

The youngest of five, Maggie had never been shy or retiring. And she knew a lie when she heard one.

"I don't think so."

Taking her hand, Maggie pushed the door to Savannah's room open again and drew a surprised Savannah back inside. Temporarily at loose ends since her move back into her parents' house, Maggie had volunteered to help Rosita with the housekeeping chores in the main house. She'd been on her way to the master bedroom when she'd stumbled into Savannah.

Maggie indicated the bed to Savannah as she made her way into the bathroom. "Why don't you lie down for a minute and I'll get you a cold compress?" It was an instruction, not a question.

Savannah glanced at her watch. It was already late and she had work to do. "No, I—"

"Your eyes are all swollen and red." Maggie's voice rose above the running water in the sink.

"You really don't want to have anyone see you looking like that, do you?"

Wringing out the washcloth, she walked back into the bedroom. She looked expectantly at Savannah, who gave in and sat down on the bed. With a gentle hand, Maggie pushed her back until she was laying down, then placed the cloth across her forehead.

"They'll ply you with a lot of useless questions you don't want to deal with right now."

Savannah watched her from beneath the cloth. "But you're not going to?" she asked suspiciously.

"I don't have to ask questions. I have a strong suspicion."

"Like your mother? Visions?"

Maggie laughed as she looked around the room. The decor was cheery and made her think of Savannah. But there were no framed photographs hanging on the wall, no candid shots propped up against the lamps or carelessly left on the bureau or tables. Weren't there people in her life she wanted to remember?

"Only the kind of 'visions' I see with my own eyes, right in front of me. But this isn't very extraordinary. A blind man could see it."

By 'this' Savannah had an uneasy feeling Maggie meant her reaction to Cruz and his last visit.

Still, she feigned ignorance. Maybe she was wrong. "See what?"

"That there's something going on between you and my brother." Moving her head, Savannah raised a corner of the washcloth to see if Maggie was about to censure her. Maggie's expression told her otherwise. "I'm all for it, personally. It's about time Cruz had someone in his life."

Now that was funny, Savannah thought. "From what I hear, Cruz has a great many 'someones' in his life." *Too many,* she added silently.

But there was a difference, Maggie thought. Hadn't Cruz made Savannah realize that? No, of course not. He was a man, and men had this ridiculous notion that women just understood what was left unspoken. They didn't realize that sometimes words were needed.

"Those are just tourists, passing through. I'm talking about someone who's interested in settling down, settling in." And Savannah, Maggie sensed, was a nester.

Savannah bit her lower lip. "I'm not interested in that."

Maggie didn't believe Savannah for a minute. She'd seen the way the two had looked at each other. Seen the way they'd interacted—or not interacted, as was now the case. There was too much smoke for there not to be a fire.

Maggie raised a brow. "Oh?"

Savannah sighed, wishing she could somehow disappear beneath the cloth the way a child thought she disappeared from view just because her eyes were shut and she couldn't see anyone. "Your brother isn't a wild mustang I intend to break."

The stereotypical description surprised Maggie. From everything she'd heard and observed, she would have expected more insight from Savannah. "Then you haven't been paying attention to him, or his work."

"His work?"

Maggie touched a little figurine of a stallion, rearing on his hind legs on the shelf next to the window. She found it interesting that Savannah had left this knickknack that was already in the room when she moved in. Interesting and telling.

"Cruz doesn't 'break' mustangs, he gentles them. Brings their best side out, their 'gifts,' if you will." *The way he might with the right kind of woman,* Maggie thought. "The way I always saw it, he was doing the horse a favor."

"Nice sentiment." But it still didn't have anything to do with her, Savannah thought. Or with them.

"*True* sentiment," Maggie corrected.

It looked as if she was going to have to spell this out for Savannah, Maggie decided. Obviously, the woman had been hurt. Cruz was not the most easygoing man, even if he gave that impression. Inside him there was a cauldron of swirling emotions. Sometimes, they burned.

"Cruz has been drop-dead beautiful and pigheadedly stubborn all of his life and all at the same time. He also has a chip on his shoulder," Maggie added matter-of-factly.

Savannah laughed shortly. "I hadn't noticed."

"The Twin Towers would be easier to miss. To him, the world is divided into 'them' and 'us.'" Maggie figured she wasn't saying anything that Savannah probably didn't already know, or at least suspect. "He wants to show 'them' that he's every bit as good as they are."

"He is." It had never occurred to Savannah that Cruz had any reason to feel inferior. He certainly didn't behave as if he was.

"Yes, he is," Maggie agreed. "But in his heart, he's not sure."

Maggie had realized that about her brother a long time ago, piecing together offhanded words and fragments of scenarios over the years. It made her heart ache that Cruz should feel this way. But she'd figured out the origins of the sentiment, at least in part.

"He's been used by those same ladies who flock to him." She saw the question in Savannah's eyes as she looked at her beneath the compress. "Used as a trophy. Their one wild affair with 'The Cowboy,'" Maggie elaborated. "The blame belongs to both of them—to Cruz and to the women." Her brother certainly wasn't lily-white in this. But he was her brother, and she loved him dearly. "But it soured him when he realized that was all he was to them—a trophy, a pelt. A thing."

"You mean he was idealistic once?"

Maggie smiled. He'd probably have her head for saying this. But some things were more important than supporting his machismo. "Yes, and under all that bravado, Cruz still is. You just have to reach in far enough to get to it."

"Provided he wants to have it reached."

Maggie lifted one shoulder carelessly before letting it drop again. "Whether he thinks he does or not doesn't matter. What does is that he'd be a better person for it. And happier." She looked down at Savannah. "I think you can make him happy."

"Why would you think that? You hardly know me."

Maggie laughed. "Because I've never seen him more miserable."

Savannah sighed. She had a headache, but it wasn't impairing her reasoning. This was a broader leap than she felt up to making. "You're going to have to explain that."

"If you didn't count, he'd be behaving the way he always does—cocky, self-assured. In other words, he'd be Cruz."

"And he's not Cruz now?"

Maggie shook her head. "Not the Cruz I know. He's changed since you came to live at the ranch."

For a second, Savannah remained where she was, hiding behind a bit of blue, plush terry cloth. And then she made a decision. There was no doubt in her mind that Maggie knew about the pregnancy. Everyone on the ranch probably did. But parentage was another matter.

Savannah pulled the washcloth from her forehead and sat up. "That's because—"

Maggie nodded, wanting to spare her. "I know all about the baby."

"Yes, but—"

"And that it's Cruz's."

Surprise stole her words away for a beat before allowing them to form. "He told you?"

"He didn't have to. I told you—I watch, I observe. The pieces aren't all that difficult to put together. My mother suspected it first, but then my mother always suspects things, and she's only right part of the time." Maggie grinned. "Not that she'd admit it." Moving a little closer to her on the bed,

Maggie placed her hand over Savannah's in silent friendship. She'd taken a liking to this woman almost from the start. In some matters, she and her brother reacted identically. "The way I see it, the question now is, how do you feel about Cruz?"

Savannah was generally open with people, but there was always a tiny edge left for self-preservation. She teetered on it now. "I honestly don't know. There are feelings, but—"

Maggie cut her off. "Sorry, not my place to ask that. And I know all about those jumbled feelings," she assured Savannah quickly. "Been there myself." Her thoughts drifted for a moment, touching warm places from the past. "More than once."

Maggie was giving her privacy, and Savannah appreciated the gesture. "The thing I am clear about," Savannah told her honestly, "is that I don't want to rope your brother in."

"That's exactly why I think you'd be perfect for him."

"You lost me."

Patiently, Maggie explained. "You don't want anything from him. He's not a trophy to you, or—forgive me—a one-night stand." It was an insulting term, but one that had fit Cruz's activities more than once. "You think of him as a person."

"He *is* a person. A very exciting person." Remembering their fateful night together, Savannah's expression softened a little. "Without a doubt, the most exciting person I've ever met."

Maggie grinned. And wouldn't his head swell if he heard that? "I wouldn't go that far. But if you feel that way about him…"

The implication was clear. If she felt that way, why wouldn't she marry him? Savannah shook her head. "I won't trap him—and that's exactly how he'll feel. If he doesn't feel that now."

Maggie knew she was interfering, but she'd already gone all this way—a few more inches weren't going to matter. Besides, when you loved someone, it wasn't interfering so much as looking out for them. Cruz had always looked after her. It was time she returned the favor.

"I believe what Cruz feels now is that you don't think he's good enough for you."

"What? How did he get that idea? I never said—"

"You have to remember that you're Vanessa's friend. That puts you in a completely different class. The same class as all those women who came to his bed so willingly just for the thrill of it." Maggie smiled. "He doesn't think I know about them, but I do."

Upset, Savannah hardly heard what Maggie was saying. It had never occurred to her that Cruz would misunderstand the reason for her refusal. "I can't have him thinking that."

"No," Maggie agreed. "You can't." Satisfied, she rose and took the washcloth from Savannah's hand. "You look much better now."

Savannah glanced toward the mirror hanging over the bureau. Her complexion was no longer pallid. Color was returning to her face, ushered in by what Maggie had shared with her.

"Then I'd better go." Savannah smiled her gratitude to the other woman for taking the time to talk with her. "Thanks."

Maggie inclined her head, the way Savannah had often seen Cruz do. "Don't mention it."

Savannah didn't waste time on breakfast. Her stomach in a new kind of knot, she knew she couldn't eat anyway. Instead, she went out to find Cruz. She wasn't sure just what she would say to him, only that she had to clear the air. She had to clear away the ridiculous assumption that she had turned him down because she felt she was too good for him or the life he had to offer.

She'd come from money and knew firsthand that it didn't buy happiness. Happiness was a gift.

Do better? How could you do any better than to marry the person you loved?

Cruz wasn't at the corral where she normally

saw him. The enclosure was empty. Disappointment bit into her as she looked helplessly around.

"Are you looking for someone?"

She turned around to see Ruben approaching
her. His smile was gentle, kind. With very little
imagination, she could see him as the father she'd
always wanted.

"I'm looking for Cruz—"

Ruben shook his head apologetically. "He's not
here. He's training the horse in the meadow today.
To see how he does without confinements."

Murphy's law, she thought, frustrated. "Do you
know when he'll be back?"

"Not until much later. I could send one of the
hands to get him—"

No, she didn't want to make Cruz feel as if she
was summoning him. He already misunderstood
too much. "No, that's all right. It can wait." Turning, she began walking away.

"I'll let him know you were looking for him,"
he called after her.

"Thank you."

Savannah banked down her impatience. She
wanted to ride out to Cruz, but there was her own
work to see to. She wasn't about to take
of the Fortunes by being lax. She knew they probably wouldn't mind, but she would. So she went

back to the house, to the office on the first floor, and did her work. Or tried to.

Every so often, she caught herself gazing out the window, but Cruz never returned. His father was right. Apparently, Cruz was gone for the day.

Maggie's words ringing in her ears, Savannah grew more restless as the day progressed.

How could he possibly have thought that she drew some sort of caste line between them? That she had refused his proposal because she thought herself better than him?

Just how stupid was this man? Couldn't he tell how she felt? That he made her weak in the knees. That waking up each morning with him beside her was something she held as an unattainable dream? That she was in anguish because she had to turn him down, even though she had it in her power to make her dream come true, at least physically?

But it was emotional, not physical, commitment she wanted. She wanted Cruz to love her first, then propose—not marry her out of some sense of duty and honor. Duty and honor were all well and good for a soldier, but not for a husband. At least, not as a primary motive for marriage.

She wanted him to be as crazy about her as...well, as she was about him.

She sighed. Okay, it was out, if only in her own mind. She was crazy about him. In love with him.

So much in love that she was afraid even to acknowledge it for fear that she'd disintegrate under its heat.

Damn it, he should be grateful to her for being so stupidly noble when another woman would…

Eventually, another woman *would,* she thought sadly. Blinking back tears, Savannah turned from the computer screen. Another woman would grace his bed, bear his children, hear the words that she wanted to hear.

Another woman, but not her.

"That's right, make yourself nuts," she muttered accusingly to herself.

"Why would you want to do that?"

Swiveling around in her chair, Savannah saw Vanessa looking at her as she walked in, a bemused smile on her lips.

"I don't, it's just that—" Sighing, she shook her head. It was far too complicated to explain, and she was tired. "Never mind."

Vanessa didn't press Savannah for an explanation. "Devin and I just wanted to ask you if you'd like to come out with us for dinner. There isn't going to be anyone home tonight, and I didn't want you to be alone."

Perfect, Savannah thought. There'd be no one to question where she'd been if she rode out to see

Cruz. "Don't worry about me. I'll just have a sandwich here, thanks."

Vanessa frowned. "When I hired you, I didn't want you to think I did so with intentions of chaining you to the desk."

"No chaining," Savannah assured her. "I like working."

"You never did listen to anyone." Vanessa looked at her watch. "Well, Devin's waiting. I'll see you in the morning."

Savannah nodded, debating whether or not to say anything. But if she couldn't trust Vanessa, who could she trust?

"Vanessa?"

At the door, her friend stopped to look at her. "Yes?"

"Do you know where Cruz is?" she asked innocently. "I haven't seen him all day—"

"He's probably gone to his cabin by now."

"His cabin?" For some reason, she'd thought he lived in his parents' house.

Vanessa nodded. "He has his own place not too far from Rosita and Ruben's house. Just due south of here. Maybe about five miles. Maybe less." Thunder rumbled. "We'd better get going if we want to reach town before the storm breaks. I hate driving on these roads in the rain." She touched

Savannah's face. "Anything you want me to bring back?"

Savannah made a face. "If you value our friendship, don't talk about food."

"Sorry."

Savannah heard Vanessa laugh as she hurried away down the hall.

Nine

The next ten minutes felt as if they were being dragged by on a wagon with square wheels. Containing her impatience, Savannah waited for about ten minutes in her office. She didn't want to run into Vanessa and then have to explain where she was going.

It was just something she knew she had to do if she were ever to be at peace again.

When she was fairly certain that she would safely avoid contact with anyone who felt entitled to ask questions, Savannah hurried to the stables. Pixie Dust was in her stall, put away for the night. Ryan had made a point of letting her know that the horse was hers to use for as long as she remained on the ranch. It made Savannah feel less of an outsider, more like a member of the family. It helped, belonging.

She thought of Cruz. How long had he felt like an outsider, like someone just looking in? Her heart went out to him.

Although some of the others on the ranch used

a Jeep to get around, she found riding a horse preferable in these surroundings. And she already dearly loved Pixie Dust.

"I know you thought you were in for the day, and I'm sorry to have to take you out on such a gloomy night," she murmured as she saddled the horse. "But this'll just take a little while, I promise. Less, if I lose my nerve and turn back."

Clouds dipped in soot lined the sky as she led the mare out. And the sky grew darker and more ominous as she rode in the direction of Cruz's cabin. Never having been there, Savannah was relying solely on Vanessa's nebulous directions that the cabin was due south of the main house.

The sensible thing to do was to wait until morning. But she wasn't feeling very sensible. She had to see Cruz, and it had to be tonight. The words were hot on her tongue and she wanted to say them before she lost her nerve. Things would only continue to grow worse between them until she cleared this up.

Before she was halfway there, it started to pour.

The rain didn't bother him, but Cruz was concerned about the effect the storm would have on Quicksilver, the stallion he'd been training these past few weeks. The animal was already skittish. Cruz's own horse was well trained to take sudden loud noises in stride, but Quicksilver hadn't come that far yet. This could be a setback.

The weather had changed suddenly, bringing with it the promise of a storm. Now he wished he hadn't remained in the meadow so long. But he and Quicksilver had finally begun to bond, and he hadn't wanted to stop. Bonding was the first really strong step in mastering a horse, and he knew from experience that it was an elusive thing that needed to be strengthened once it materialized.

Cruz rode quickly to the stables, anxious to get the horse in before the storm broke.

"It's okay, Silver. It's only noise, nothing else." The soothing tone of his voice helped keep the animal calm.

Hellfire pawed the ground, obviously not happy about having to stand around and wait while Cruz tended to the other horse. Cruz smiled to himself. The animals were behaving just like jealous women.

He thought of his own reaction to Dallas when the man had been dancing with Savannah. Maybe the emotion wasn't restricted to women, he mused.

"I'm going as fast as I can. Your turn will come," he told Hellfire.

With long, even strokes, he groomed the gray's coat until he was certain that the animal was at peace and that none of the headway they'd made today was undone by the whimsy of weather.

Satisfied he'd done all he could, Cruz led Hellfire back out into the rain. "Sorry, can't be helped. If it makes you feel any better, I'm getting wetter than you are."

Swinging into the saddle, he turned the stallion south and headed for home.

From a distance, he saw what looked like a glimmer of light coming from his cabin as he approached it. Cruz wondered if it was some trick being played by the rain. Was he imagining lights in the windows? He didn't remember leaving any on when he left early this morning.

Rather than stopping to investigate, he guided Hellfire toward the stable. By now, Cruz was soaked to the skin and bone-tired, but he had to tend to the horse before he could see about anything else.

Maybe he'd sleep tonight, he thought. It would be a relief if he finally could. He hadn't last night, or any of the nights before. At least, not more than an hour or two at a time. He couldn't go on like that indefinitely.

Dismounting at the stable doors, he pushed one open and led Hellfire in. "Bet you're glad today is over," he murmured to his horse. "Me, too."

And then he stopped.

Pixie Dust was in the stall that Hellfire normally occupied.

What the hell was the mare doing here? Cruz glanced toward the cabin behind him. So the light hadn't been his imagination.

"Looks like we have company, boy."

Banking down the urge to rush into the house and see if she was really there, Cruz forced himself to take care of Hellfire first. It was only fair.

Besides, he reasoned, he needed the time to pull himself together.

When the front door finally opened, Savannah jumped and stifled a gasp. She'd been waiting for Cruz for over an hour now, fidgeting as she intently watched the door. Wondering if maybe she was acting rashly and should leave. Her reaction to his entrance showed her just how close to the surface her nerves were, and what state they were in.

Not good.

She pressed her lips together. Everything she'd come to say, everything she'd diligently rehearsed on the way over here, flew out of her head the instant Cruz walked in.

Savannah looked at the puddle of water that was forming around his boots. "You're all wet."

His face impassive, Cruz shed his jacket, leaving

it on the back of a chair. He threw his hat on top
of it. Rain clung to the front of his hair.

"Happens when it's raining." His eyes slid over
her impersonally, and Savannah felt a pang deep
in her heart. "What are you doing here?"

His tone was cold. Savannah pushed on, anyway. "I thought we should talk."

He dragged his hand through his dark hair.
Drops scattered in the wake of his fingers. "I
thought we already had."

"Not enough, apparently." Flustered, she laced
her fingers together and told herself that she was
an adult, a woman, not a child fumbling with a
speech in front of her classroom. It didn't help. "I
talked to Maggie this morning."

"Oh?"

His brow raised dangerously as he pulled off his
boots and set them to the side. Like everything
else, they were soaked through. He was going to
have to polish them if he didn't want them to be
ruined, he thought, his mind bouncing around,
touching everything but the woman who was
standing in his living room. He didn't want to think
about her, had worked very hard not to think about
her all day.

He could think of nothing else.

Savannah tried again. "She said something..."
Her voice trailed off as she searched for the right

words—the ones she'd lost the moment he'd walked in, looking bigger than life and handsomer than any living man had a right to be.

Cruz gave a careless half shrug. "Maggie is always saying something." Pulling his shirttails out of his jeans, he began unbuttoning his shirt, completely ignoring her presence.

Savannah tried again, and found herself faltering. She just couldn't think right now—not when he was taking his shirt off.

Frustrated at her own inability to concentrate, Savannah sighed. "Would you not do that, please?"

He separated the last button from its hole and stared at her. His shirt hung open, framing a chest that was well muscled and hard. "Do what?"

"Get undressed while I'm talking to you."

He paused only a moment. "This is my cabin, and as you pointed out, I'm all wet. I'd like to get all dry." To prove it, he stripped off his shirt and tossed it aside. It landed on top of his hat.

"Maybe this wasn't a good idea, coming here." As a matter of fact, it was probably one of the worst ideas she'd ever had.

"Maybe it wasn't," he agreed. He didn't want her here. Didn't want Savannah intruding into his life any more than she already had. She didn't belong in his life. In his head.

But she was there.

And here.

Cruz watched in silence as Savannah walked to the door. But just as she placed her hand on the doorknob, there was a quick flash that illuminated the room as if it were day. Almost immediately, another rumble of thunder, louder and more fierce than the last, shook the cabin. The center of the storm was on top of them.

He didn't like thinking of her out on a night like this. "Maybe you'd better wait out the storm."

Angry, hurt, upset, all she wanted to do was get away from him, if not the pain. Refusing to look at Cruz, she squared her shoulders, trying to sound as disinterested as he had.

"Don't tell me what I should do," she snapped.

"Look, it's raining hard out there. I just thought you'd be better off waiting and not getting wet. But go ahead, do what you want."

"I fully intend to."

But when she opened the door, another rumble of thunder echoed, merging with the bolt of lightning that creased the sky less than a moment earlier. Like the center of a fire, everything blazed brightly for a single moment before being cast into darkness.

The lights in the cabin went out.

A velvet darkness embraced everything, without

and within. Savannah shut the door again. She couldn't see an inch in front of her. It was like being in an abyss.

"Damn." The oath was ripe and vehement as it left Cruz's lips. "The power went out," he said, more to himself than to her.

She hated the dark. She always had. "Will it go back on?"

"In the big house, yes. They've got an emergency generator. I don't."

Turning, Cruz took careful steps toward where he assumed the fireplace was. But instead, he found himself walking into something soft. Belatedly, he realized Savannah must have moved. Because of the impact, he reached for her to keep her from being thrown off balance. His hands brushed against her breasts as he grabbed her shoulders.

"Sorry."

Thin currents of electricity shot through her. "My fault," she murmured.

His chest was hard against hers. She could feel his heart beating. At least, she was fairly certain it was his heart. Hers had frozen in her chest.

Slowly, the feel of his hands on her arms penetrated. She didn't want to move out of the way. She wanted to remain just where she was, hiding behind the excuse the power failure had created.

Cruz's common sense, logic and instinct for survival all joined together and dictated that he back away and let her go. She wasn't in any danger of falling. But he was.

Yet Cruz couldn't help himself.

All the tension, all the anger and longing he'd been feeling fused and surged through his veins, demanding release.

He brought his mouth down on hers, hungry for her taste, for her sweetness. He wasn't gentle.

The air *whooshed* out of her lungs at the first hint of contact. It took her more than a minute to get her bearings, only to lose them all over again as the kiss deepened, taking her with it to a place she'd longed to go.

Reactions came faster than thoughts. Delight urged her arms around his neck, her body to his. Savannah gave herself up to the moment, knowing it was wrong. Knowing it was probably all she would have. But she had to make the most of it. It was going to have to last for a very long time.

He lingered just for a moment, absorbing the feel of her, his mouth slanting over hers with an intensity that would have surprised him if he'd been able to think. But he couldn't.

And then Cruz knew that if he didn't let her go now, he wouldn't be able to, whether he wanted to or not. He didn't like being held prisoner by his own urges. He didn't like not being in control.

The struggle cost him.

The victory cost more.

Releasing her, Cruz slid his hands from Savannah's waist. Reluctance marked every inch. "I'd better see about getting a fire going."

Her breath came in small snatches, like that of a woman who had just been saved from drowning. "I think you already have."

The muscles on his bare chest tightened as he felt her breath lightly swirling along his skin. Arousing him. "In the fireplace."

Her heart was pounding like the surf at the height of a hurricane. "I'd get out of your way, except I don't know which way to move."

That, he thought, was just the trouble. There seemed to be no way to move her out of his way. Every way he turned, she seemed to be there.

"Just stand still," he told her. "I'll do the rest."

Nervousness made her giddy, and Savannah laughed.

In the dark, the sound was seductive, Cruz thought. He shook off its effects as, hands outstretched, he found his way to the fireplace. "What?"

She remained where he had told her to stay. "Is that what you tell all your other conquests?"

"No." And then, taking out a match and squatting down, he sobered as he lingered on what she'd just said. "Is that what you think you are—a conquest?" Carefully, he felt around for kindling.

She could hear his movements. They floated to her as the thunder took a respite. Desire warred with resolve. "Wasn't I?"

He tucked the kindling between the logs, resenting the picture she was painting.

"I don't 'conquer' women. To conquer means to invade, to possess, to dominate. I don't do any of that." He struck the match against a brick; it hissed as a flame leaped into existence. He tossed it into the kindling and waited for it to take. "Women usually come to me, so I don't invade. I certainly don't own them, so there's no possessing involved. And as far as dominating..." His voice trailed off into a laugh. If anything, the women tried to dominate, attempting to impose their will on him. The flame took and spread, greedily consuming the kindling. "I enjoy women."

"And did you 'enjoy' me?" The question came in a hushed whisper.

"Very, very much." He stared into the fire for a moment, watching it grow. Just like his longing. "There, I think I've got that going now."

Like a lover, the fire's warm glow caressed his face. Savannah watched in silence as Cruz rose to his feet again, wiping his hands off on his jeans. A few drops of rain still clung to his hair.

They would be gone soon, she thought.

Silly the things a person thinks about when confronted with their own needs. And she was beginning to think hers would never be resolved.

She watched as Cruz turned toward her. Watched and felt her heart twisting in her chest. Boy or girl, her baby would be beautiful if it looked like him.

"So," he began as if everything within him wasn't begging him to take Savannah, to make love with her here on the floor of his cabin, while the wind and the forces of nature howled just outside his door, "what did you come to tell me?"

She drew her eyes away from him. "That you're wrong."

"About anything in particular, or just in general?" The soft smile on his lips faded. "Or just wrong for you?"

Savannah swung around to face him, the comment restoring all the courage she'd temporarily lost.

"You're wrong about what you're thinking. Maggie told me that she believed you thought I turned down your proposal because I felt I could—" she threw up her hands in total frustration "—Oh, God, this is so stupid, I can't even say the words." Anger crystallized her convictions. "I judge people on who they are, Cruz, not how much change they have in their pockets, or where the post office drops off their mail. And certainly not on whose photographs are in their family album.''

She was almost breathing fire. All he could think was that she was magnificent. And that he wanted her more than he wanted to wake up tomorrow morning.

"We don't have a family album," he told her evenly. "My mother keeps all her pictures in the box that held the first pair of boots she bought my father."

Semantics. She was pouring out her heart, and he was toying with words. "Whatever." She licked her bottom lip, confused, nervous. "Stop trying to mix me up."

The smile was slow and all the more sensuous for the journey. "Do I?" His eyes took hers prisoner. "Do I mix you up?"

There was no point in denying it. "Like a blender."

Because he couldn't keep his distance any longer, couldn't stand having almost the length of a room between them, Cruz crossed to her. He was a man moving toward his destiny. And his doom. It didn't matter. Nothing mattered except having her.

"And that's a bad thing?"

"Yes, it's a bad thing." But there was no conviction in her voice. "I'm used to being able to think straight." And right now, she couldn't even think, much less think straight.

Savannah wanted to back away. She wanted to tell him what she'd come to say, and then leave, before something happened. Before *he* happened. But she couldn't seem to get started. Instead, she remained where she was, watching him as he drew closer to her. Making the inches between them evaporate.

"Sometimes, thinking gets in the way. Sometimes, you have to put all that aside, and just feel."

His words were causing tidal waves in her stomach, breaking down defenses that were, at best, made of papier-mâché.

Run, damn it. Run for your life, girl. Don't just stand here, praying that he takes you in his arms again.

But she was standing. And she was praying. Because nothing else seemed to matter right now, except that she wanted him to hold her. To kiss her again, just the way he had before he'd lit the fire. And to make love with her, because her whole body was aching for his touch, for the fiery, mindless magic that she'd only felt once before. In his arms.

"I did put everything aside and just feel." Color rose to her cheeks. "Remember?"

"Yes." He smiled, feathering his fingers through her hair, framing her face. "I remember." He began lowering his mouth to hers.

The loud roll of thunder startled Savannah and she jerked, turning her head toward the sound. Cruz found himself kissing her hair. He laughed, then saw her flush in embarrassment. Something tender and protective stirred within him.

"It's only noise," he soothed, saying the same words he'd said to Quicksilver earlier.

It seemed ridiculous to react that way at her age. He probably thought she was an idiot. "I know, you're right. But it always makes me jumpy. I was afraid of thunderstorms when I was a little girl, and I guess I never completely got over it."

He'd been afraid of thunder, too, until his father had made it all go away with one of his fanciful explanations. It wasn't until years later that Cruz realized that all kids weren't fortunate enough to have a father like his.

"What did your parents tell you?"

Savannah didn't understand. "Tell me? About what?"

He smiled to himself as another crash of thunder drove Savannah further into his arms. "About thunderstorms."

She shook her head. "Nothing. I didn't tell them I was afraid."

He wondered why. As a child, he'd shared everything with his parents. "Maybe you should have. I remember this one storm we had. It felt like the wind was howling for hours. I was about five at the time, and terrified. My father found me hiding under his bed. He pulled me out and asked me what was the matter. When I told him, he just laughed, then sat me down on his lap and said, 'It's just the angels, Cruz, reminding us that they're there.'

"I asked him why they were so very noisy, and he looked at me, his face as straight as if he were reading chapter and verse out of his old family bible." Cruz's voice deepened again, imitating his father almost to a tee. "'What do you think, that they're all these tall, skinny things you see painted in books? These are angels like you and me and your uncle Pablo.'"

"Uncle Pablo?" Savannah didn't remember anyone on the ranch by that name.

"He was my father's uncle. At the time, Uncle Pablo weighed in at around two hundred and sixty pounds. I was very impressed with the comparison." His eyes glinted as he continued. "My father said, 'Those kind of angels, they make noise when they move around.'" Cruz grinned as he looked down at her, and she felt her heart melting. "I was never afraid of thunderstorms again."

"Angels," she repeated.

"Uh-huh."

"Weighing about two hundred and sixty pounds."

"About."

"I don't know about you, but that would certainly scare me."

The grin faded into something softer and even more lethal. "There are things to be afraid of in this world, Savannah, but large angels aren't one of them."

"Oh?" She felt her voice catching in her breath. "What are you afraid of? Or aren't you afraid of anything?"

Very slowly, he began to undo the tiny buttons at her throat. "Oh, I'm afraid of things all right."

A moment ago, she'd been close to shivering. Now it seemed unbearably hot in the small cabin. Her eyes held his, afraid to look anywhere else.

"Like?"

"Like this moment." Two more buttons were released from captivity. Very slowly, Cruz dipped just the tips of his fingers inside the space they created, barely gliding over the softest hint of skin. "You."

"You're afraid of me?" His fingertips burned as they skimmed along her skin. She could hardly force the words from her lips.

"Terrified." The word whispered along her skin, tantalizing her.

"Why?"

Very gently, he drew the rest of the blouse apart. Savannah wasn't wearing a bra. His smile was slow, sensual and completely bone-melting as it washed over her.

"You figure it out."

Ten

His eyes touched her face. "I haven't been able to get you out of my mind."

"You don't have to feel guilty. I relieved you of blame and responsibility."

It wasn't that simple. Guilt he could deal with. You either made amends, or, if that wasn't possible, you put it out of your mind. You put it behind you. But he couldn't seem to do that with her, no matter how hard he tried. Just when he thought he had succeeded, she would suddenly, and with no reason, turn up again in his mind. To linger there, tormenting him.

"Guilt has nothing to do with it. I keep remembering the way you looked that night." Even mentioning it brought the scene vividly back to him. Cruz felt his gut tightening in anticipation. His eyes on hers, he skimmed his fingertips up along her sides until his hands cupped her. "The way you felt."

His rough hands rubbed along her tender flesh,

and Savannah bit back a moan of half pain, half pleasure. And all desire.

"The way you tasted." He pressed a languid kiss to her throat, his lips sliding ever so slowly down the long white column. Cruz felt her pulse there beating erratically beneath his mouth. He didn't know why that excited him so much. It just did.

And it made him want more.

His emotions exposed, his feelings unguarded, he allowed a confession to slip through. "I've wanted to make love with you again. Badly."

That was all it was, she told herself. Lovemaking. Physical. Nothing else. No matter how much she wanted it to be more, it wasn't. She had to remember that and be satisfied with what she had. What she might share with him tonight.

Her mouth curved in amusement and pleasure. "I doubt very much if you have ever made love *badly* in your life, Cruz."

The light in her eyes told him she was teasing. He had no idea why that felt so intimate to him.

He laughed, kissing her mouth quickly, nipping her lower lip. The laughter faded, drowned out by desire so large, so unwieldy that it threatened to swallow him up whole without leaving a trace to even mark where he'd existed.

"Then I'll try not to start now," he promised softly a second before his mouth covered hers.

His arms around her, holding her as closely as was humanly possible without having them merge into one, Cruz felt Savannah sigh against him. And surrender.

Urges rushed out—urges that had only temporarily retreated below the surface. Needs rattled the bars of restraint he'd been trying to construct. Bars that were as useless as a sieve was to hold back rainwater.

His mouth hot on hers, Cruz kissed her over and over again, growing that much more entrenched, that much more lost in her.

It didn't please him that Savannah had preyed on his mind like this. That she continued to prey on it even while he held her, even while he made love with her.

He ached for her even as he tried to ease the ache.

No other woman had ever done this to him, had ever done more than evoke a passing smile from him after he'd had her. Yet Savannah stirred his hunger, his passions and an overwhelming, driving need to have her again. And again after that.

It gave her an advantage over him.

Cruz didn't want to think about that now. He didn't want common sense or logic to rear its head and interfere with this exquisite moment that the storm and fate had conspired to hand him. She was here now, and he wanted her.

Maybe this time, after he'd had her, she would fade from his mind like all the others.

Like a flame rushing along a fuse of dynamite, heat rushed over her. Heat so all consuming that she vaguely thought one of the sparks from the fireplace had leaped out of the hearth and landed on her.

But it wasn't a spark. It was Cruz. Cruz's touch, Cruz's kiss. Cruz's body pressed so urgently against hers, hardening so provocatively.

She hadn't thought it possible to want him more than she already did. But it was, because the hunger she felt was ravenous. There was no containing it. She didn't even try.

No longer shy, no longer withdrawn, Savannah cleaved to him, her own body thrilling at the reunion. All thoughts of being strong and resisting died instantly. All she wanted was to feel alive again, just one more time.

The clothes that were still left on their bodies quickly flew away in a flurry of eager hands urgently pushing away barriers. Eager to claim what was there. To reexplore, to reunite. To seize the moment before it was gone, and sanity returned.

Right now it, and everything else, was a million miles away. Only the two of them were here.

There was a part of Cruz that wanted to savor these feelings for all they were worth because they were so unique. But Cruz was at war with himself. His blood surging hot, he had to restrain himself from taking her quickly, the way everything within him begged him to. He wanted to make love to Savannah with complete abandon before something happened to rob him of this sensation. To steal it away from him. To steal *her* away from him.

The thought that he wanted her this urgently, this all-consumingly scared the hell out of him. Until this moment, he had always prided himself on retaining control.

He couldn't claim that anymore.

But Cruz stopped a moment before he was going to take her. Savannah looked up at him in the firelight. "What's the matter?"

Cruz wanted to tell her everything he was feeling. But he'd never shared this remote corner of his soul. Never allowed anyone to come so close to him that he feared being without them. Even with his own family, there were small fences, small recessed paths where he hadn't let them follow. Telling her what he was feeling right at this moment—needy, confused, aching—would allow Savannah into a place he had never allowed anyone else to enter. It risked too much, exposed too much. He needed to be self-contained. Loving this way had too many consequences.

Locking the inner door that had opened just a crack, Cruz framed her face and brought his mouth down to hers. "Nothing."

She tasted the word before she heard it. And if she was going to protest that she knew he was lying, that there was something bothering him, she never got the opportunity. The tender assault he'd mounted blotted out her mind.

Gently pushing her onto the handwoven rug before the fireplace, Cruz reacquainted himself with every inch of her. Instead of the darkness of the stable, he had the light of the fire to show him the way.

He made love with her with every fiber of his being, wanting to lose himself in her, to outrace any thoughts that could hold him back, threatened to destroy this temporary paradise.

"You're beautiful," he whispered, his hands creating wondrous feelings that leaped into existence within her.

How many times had he said that to other women as he made love with them? she wondered. It didn't matter. Tonight, she'd pretend that she was the first. And the last. She'd pretend to believe him.

Each movement in response to him, each noise of pleasure, of desire that escaped from Savannah only fueled his craving for her. He knew he wasn't her first lover—that there had been someone before him. But she made him feel as if he were her first. And made him wish with all his heart that he was.

He'd never wanted that before, either. To be the first to take a woman, the first to make her feel like a woman. But he'd want to share that precious moment with Savannah.

If he couldn't be her first, then he would be her most memorable. He wanted at least that much.

He wanted everything.

He wanted.

Her belly began to quiver as his lips started to forge a long, languid, seductive trail along her body. As the fire's warm glow bathed her, he kissed the instep of her foot, her ankle, the sensitive skin behind her knee. He worked his way up along her body, discovering places that brought a sweet, sensual rush through her veins, a quickening in her loins.

It was magic.

Twisting and turning beneath him as sensations flashed through her, bringing her up and over, then back to earth, only to start the journey all over again, Savannah burned for him. She wanted only to be his in the complete, final sense of the word.

Unable to keep the longing under restraint, she raised her hands to him. "I want you," she whispered.

He'd heard the words before. Had said the words before. But had never felt them in his soul as he did now.

Fighting feelings that had no place in his plans, in the life he had laid out for himself, Cruz gathered Savannah to him roughly. He was angry that he couldn't divorce himself from all this, the way he usually could.

It was physical, only physical, he told himself. She didn't have a hold on him.

But she did.

His body over hers, Cruz seized her mouth and lowered himself until he filled her. Her legs encircled his hips, closing around him. Urging him on.

A face like an angel, a body like sin. The words echoed in his brain as he surrendered himself to the feeling battering at him.

To the feeling, and to her.

The ride was wild, erratic and timeless. Capturing his goal, or being captured up by it—he couldn't be sure—Cruz could only let it all happen.

Ecstasy released a web of euphoria that blanketed him.

He sank to earth with a smile on his face, and listened to his heart beat against hers. It was a comforting sensation, a comforting sound.

He felt her breath along his face, felt her chest move slowly up and down beneath his. Belatedly, he realized that she was pinned beneath him.

"I'm crushing you." But as he began to shift away from her, Savannah's arms went around him.

"Not yet," she entreated. "Just a little longer."

The request undid him. Desire, fresh and reborn, sprang up in the wake of the contentment that had, only a second before, spread over him. How the hell could she manage that—to make him want her all over again so quickly? What was it about her that was so different, so compelling?

He raised himself up on his elbows and looked down into her face. Definitely a face like an angel. As for her body... He felt her move. Felt himself hardening. Felt his mouth curve.

"Don't ask for much, do you?"

She could feel him wanting her, and knowing that made her soar. A smile beginning from the innermost core worked its way out, pervading her body, her heart. She smiled in invitation.

"I try not to."

He nipped at her lower lip, catching it between his teeth and suckling it before anointing her chin with his tongue. She moved ever more urgently beneath him. Arousal gripped him more firmly.

Cruz watched in amusement as Savannah's eyes widened. He laughed softly at the surprise he saw there. He kissed her neck, then whispered against her ear.

"What can I say? You are an inspiration."

With no thought of looking back, she gave herself up to him.

Savannah stirred. Something warm was draped over her. Cruz? She opened her eyes and saw that it was only a blanket. He wasn't next to her.

Sadness shot long, tenuous threads through her as she shifted to her other side, ready to get up. Cruz was sitting on her other side, between her and the fireplace. Looking at her.

What was he thinking? She couldn't read his expression. Was he regretting what had happened? Or was it the baby inside her he regretted? Awake, without the magical mist of lovemaking to mute her thoughts, uneasiness found its home within her again.

Blinking, she tried to focus on something other than the fact that she was completely nude beneath the blanket. And that he was the same, without one. He seemed utterly unselfconscious, despite not having a stitch on.

He was magnificent, she thought.

"What time is it?"

What would it be like, he mused, to be married? To be married to her? He'd seen plenty of marriages, both happy and not, but he'd never cast himself in the role of a husband, a father. It had just never occurred to him to think along those lines.

But now there was a woman—a woman with his child in her belly—and he thought about it. All through the night, as she lay beside him, sleeping, he thought about it.

Would it change him?

Of course, it would change him. It would change everything. But would he mind so much, if it were with her? He honestly didn't know.

She was looking at him, and he realized that she'd asked a question and was waiting for an answer.

"Late." And then he shrugged, a bemused smile working its way forward. "Or early, depending on your way of looking at things." He glanced toward the front window. It was still dark outside. "It stopped raining."

Feeling awkward, Savannah sat up and gathered the blanket around her. She'd stayed too long. "I should be getting back."

He caught her wrist, restraining her. Savannah

looked at him, puzzled. Afraid to entertain hopes that insisted on springing up.

"You could stay the rest of the night. Ride back with me in the morning."

She couldn't tell by his tone if the invitation was sincere, or if he was just extending it because of his damnable sense of duty again. She pushed the envelope a little. "Do you want me to?"

He released her wrist. "It'd be safer."

Savannah drew herself up on her knees, the blanket tucked around her like a colorful toga. "That's not what I asked."

What was it that she wanted from him? He was trying, wasn't he? He'd offered to marry her, hadn't he? Why did she insist on prodding him, on probing his mind? "No, but it's what I answered."

Savannah sank back on her heels. "Yes, it is." And she had her answer in that. Dragging her hand through her hair, she sighed and made up her mind. "I'd better go." Rising, she held the blanket tightly against her as she began to pick up her clothes.

He didn't want her out there, alone. People got lost riding around in the dark. Angry at her refusal, he snapped at her. "I said I'd take you back in the morning."

His anger provoked her own. With her clothes hugged close to her, she glared at him. "I'm not a library book you have to return to the shelf. You don't have to 'take' me anywhere.''

Just who the hell did he think he was—her disgruntled, reluctant guardian angel? She didn't need to be protected, or taken care of. There was only one thing she wanted from him, and he apparently couldn't give her that.

She tossed her hair over her bare shoulder. "I'm very capable of getting around by myself. I found your place in the dark, didn't I? I can find my way back just fine, thank you very much.''

Incensed, Cruz rose to his feet, unfazed by his nakedness. He fought the urge to shake some sense into her head.

"Why do you have to be so stubborn?'' he shouted at her.

"I don't know. Maybe it's the company I keep.''

Suddenly hearing herself, Savannah bit her lip. With effort, she subdued the anger that threatened to overwhelm her. This wasn't going to get them anywhere, and it wasn't the kind of ending she wanted to the evening they'd just spent.

"Look, I didn't come here for this. To yell and be yelled at. I just came to tell you that I wasn't turning down your proposal because of any absurd notion that I could 'do better' than you.'' Her heart was in her eyes as she looked at him, admitting more than her words did. "I really couldn't. No woman could."

If she felt that way, why wasn't she accepting his proposal? He didn't really want to get married, but he had helped to create this child and it deserved a name, a home.

"Then I don't understand—"

Was he that blind? That insensitive? "I don't want you to marry me because you have to. These are the nineties. Nobody *has* to get married anymore."

"They do if they have a sense of responsibility."

"I am not a responsibility, Cruz." *I'm a person.* "The baby is not a responsibility—"

Sarcasm twisted his mouth. "Several statutes of the law would disagree with you."

She wasn't interested in the law, in fine points hammered out by opposing lawyers. She was interested in feelings. She'd felt guilty and worthless, watching her parents go through the confining charade of a loveless marriage for the very reasons he was now attempting to drive home.

Weary, she surrendered a point. "Fine. If it makes you feel any better, you can contribute to the baby's support."

"Checks?" he asked sarcastically.

She was tired, and he was haggling. Her temper

frayed. "Cash if you wish." Exasperated, she threw up one hand. The blanket slipped a little and she yanked it back into place. "Ponies, colored beads, rocks, whatever you want, I don't care."

"What about seeing the baby?"

That had never been in dispute. "Any time you want. I intend to tell the baby who his or her father is. You won't be a secret." She'd never intended to withhold his identity from her child.

She looked around for somewhere to change. There had to be a room beyond this one. Seeing a doorway, she turned toward it.

"Savannah."

She looked at him over her shoulder. "What?"

"Don't go yet."

The request was tendered in a softer tone, but she was having trouble getting a grip on her roller-coastering emotions. And looking at him like that was hard on her. Because, angry or not, she wanted him again. Would always want him.

"Why?" she demanded. "Because you want to yell at me some more?"

"No." He crossed to her and laid a hand on her arm, not to restrain her but to entreat her. "Because I want to make love with you some more."

"I was just going to get dressed—"

He took her clothes from her, dropping them to

the floor. "You can get dressed later. Your clothes aren't going anywhere."

And neither was she, she thought. Still, she knew she shouldn't be giving in this easily "But I—"

Very gently, he took her hands in his. The blanket sank to the floor. "Anyone ever tell you that you talk too much?"

Desire rose, as urgent, as demanding as the first time. Perhaps even more, goaded by the knowledge that forever loomed on the horizon and it was barren because there was no sign of him in it.

"No, you're the first."

"Good." His arms closed around her. "I like being the first."

Savannah stayed.

Eleven

When Savannah finally returned to the main house, the sun had been up for some time. She wondered if anyone had noticed that she was missing. The house was huge enough for the others to assume that she was somewhere else within the multi-room structure.

Vanessa and Devin being newlyweds, Savannah doubted either would notice she wasn't there. And as for Claudia and Matthew, they had enough on their minds, with the strain the kidnapping was putting on them, without wondering what had become of the ranch's new bookkeeper.

Cruz leaned forward on his horse. "You're blushing," he whispered.

He found it intriguing that the woman who aroused his passion so fully and fed it so well could turn an endearing shade of pink because she was returning from a night of lovemaking.

"I just don't want them thinking that I, that we..."

"What does it matter what anyone thinks?" He

had always acted according to his own set of rules, not anyone else's. "You are over twenty-one and your own person," he reminded her. "If you want to make love from now until Christmas, it's not anyone's business but your own."

"Mine and the doctors who'd be treating me after I collapsed from exhaustion," Savannah added dryly.

He was right, of course. It was her business. Hers and his. But she wasn't the type to live in a vacuum, and other people's opinions did matter. At least, the opinions of people she liked.

Ruben had already been up for hours and was hard at work when he saw his son and Savannah ride in. Pausing, he smiled to himself as he watched them approach.

They looked good together, he thought, she with her hair the color of sun-kissed gold and he with his the color of midnight. Their children would be beautiful when they came.

All that was needed was for his son to open his eyes and see what was in front of him for the taking. Not dreams that might not happen, but reality that could.

Even from where she was, Savannah could see a wide smile lifting Ruben's features, making him look younger. She could detect a little of Cruz in the older man, or was that the other way around?

Ruben said nothing to them, only nodded. But Savannah had the definite impression that he was pleased to see them together.

It was a far cry from the way her parents would have reacted had they seen her with Cruz. Though there was no outward display of affection from them, she was their daughter, and thus, in their eyes, an extension of them—of the family name. Certain things were not permitted and were severely frowned on. That included fraternizing with the help.

The word *fraternizing* made her smile briefly.

Because of her parents, she understood Cruz's feelings about being prejudged and found lacking simply because of an accident of birth. She had known people like that, lived with people like that. People who judged others by family tree, by station, by the size of a bank account or an address, rather than by the only thing that mattered: their true inner worth.

But she was not her parents' daughter in anything but genetic composition. She had her own rules, her own heart to follow.

Except this time, Savannah thought. She couldn't go where her heart wanted her to.

Aside from a nod in greeting, Cruz said nothing to his father as he dismounted. He looked at Savannah. "Maybe I'll see you later." He stepped back as she dismounted, then took the reins from her hand. "I'll take care of the horse. You go on."

She'd already told him that she was late for work, and Cruz didn't want her getting into trouble on his account. It was his fault they were as late as they were, he thought. And hers for being so damn desirable. She'd spurred him on to a greater level of endurance and performance than he'd ever dreamed of achieving. There was something about the woman that left him forever wanting more.

And that wasn't good.

Savannah nodded her thanks as she surrendered Pixie Dust's reins. She made no response to his comment about seeing her later. Though he had been the one to say it, she felt it was probably just a throwaway line. She didn't want to seem as if she were eager to be with him again.

Right. As if the man couldn't have guessed from what had happened last night and this morning, Savannah thought sarcastically. An idiot would have been able to figure that out, and Cruz was far from stupid.

If only...

There was and would be no "if only," and she was just going to have to make her peace with that, Savannah upbraided herself. The fact that she now knew she was in love with him only strengthened her resolve not to marry Cruz and ruin his life.

Though it might never even be mentioned, Cruz would never forgive her for that, and neither would she.

Without a backward glance, she hurried away from him and toward the house.

There was a moving van parked in the driveway. The driver, a short, well-muscled man, was just loading something in through the rear doors as she approached. Devin's car was parked several feet in front of the van. Behind his car was the one that Vanessa drove.

Realizing just how late she was, Savannah hurried into the house and almost collided with Vanessa.

Vanessa grabbed both Savannah's hands to steady her. "So there you are, finally," she declared, breathless from running around. "Out for an early morning ride?"

Savannah started to correct the lie, then decided to leave it alone. There was no point in telling Vanessa that she'd spent the night with Cruz. Vanessa wouldn't understand how she could do that and still refuse to marry him. It would make no sense to her friend.

Sometimes, Savannah thought, it barely made sense to her.

"It was so pretty this morning, after the storm,"

Savannah said evasively, leaving Vanessa to draw her own conclusions.

Seeming preoccupied, Vanessa nodded as her eyes swept over two large boxes that had yet to be loaded into the van. Turning, she smiled warmly at Savannah. "I didn't want to go without saying goodbye."

The word had such a final, dismissive sound to it. Savannah had never realized how much she hated it before. "Goodbye?"

"Yes. Well, it's more like 'so long,' but you know what I mean." She laughed. "You forgot, didn't you? I can understand. Being with Cruz will do that to anyone." She shifted the conversation quickly. "Today's the day Devin and I are finally moving to his place in San Antonio."

It all came back to her now. She'd completely forgotten about it last night when she'd gone to see Cruz. And after she saw him, everything had slipped her mind.

Savannah felt an overwhelming pang taking hold. Vanessa was leaving. Granted, over the last few weeks she'd made friends with many of the people who were involved in keeping the Double Crown running so efficiently, but it was Vanessa's presence that she treasured. She was going to sorely miss seeing Vanessa every day.

Just when she was getting used to the way things were, they changed on her.

"You're right," Savannah admitted. "I did forget—"

Vanessa took her hands in both of hers. "Oh, don't look so sad. I'm going to San Antonio, not outer space. I'll still be coming back to the ranch. We'll still get together."

Savannah knew that Vanessa believed what she was saying. But between her new husband and her work as a psychologist, not to mention setting up housekeeping in San Antonio, Vanessa was going to be extremely busy. The pace would leave little time for visiting.

"And you," Vanessa said pointedly, still holding her hands as if she were waiting to extract a promise from Savannah, "can always come out to our place and see San Antonio."

Savannah had had more than enough of large cities. Life on the Double Crown suited her far better now. "I've seen San Antonio. This is nicer."

Vanessa slipped an arm around Savannah's shoulders. "You can't beat it for peacefulness," Vanessa agreed. "And almost anywhere you ride, there's a view that makes you want to cry—"

"What's this about crying?" Devin asked, coming up behind them. He laid a hand on each woman's shoulder.

Laughing, Vanessa turned her head to look at him. "Nothing. You wouldn't understand." She inclined her head toward Savannah, pretending to share a secret in a stage whisper. "Men never understand about tears."

"Yes, we do. It's a woman's deadliest weapon." Affection graced Devin's eyes as he looked at his wife. "She uses it to get her way."

Vanessa shivered. "That's politically incorrect, my love."

"But not without a germ of truth." Another warm glance passing between them, he kissed the top of Vanessa's head.

Savannah felt her chest tighten in envy. She was happy for Vanessa, for both of them. But it would have been nice if...

There it was again. *If.* The word was going to be the death of her.

Devin glanced at his watch. "We'd better get going, Vanessa."

She nodded, but made no effort to move. "In a minute." She looked at Devin. "I just want to talk to Savannah before we leave."

The mover angled a dolly under the last of the boxes in the hall, then headed out. Devin followed behind him. "I'll see if they've loaded all five hundred pounds of your clothing into the van yet."

"Smart aleck." Vanessa tossed her head. "There are only fifty."

Devin's look shifted to Savannah. "She has a gift for understatement."

"Only when I tell you how much I love you," Vanessa pointed out. "Now get out of here." She waited until Devin walked out the door before turning back to Savannah. The amused expression on Savannah's face caught her off guard. "What?"

"You two are perfect for each other, you know that?" Savannah said. It was true: there was affection in every word that passed between the couple.

"You think?" Vanessa poked her tongue in her cheek and her eyes shone. "And so are you and Cruz."

Savannah sighed. She'd gotten very little rest last night and even less sleep. She didn't feel up to a discussion on this again. "Don't start."

"Oh, but I have to," Vanessa teased. "I won't have another chance for a few days." Suddenly, Vanessa grew serious. "Listen to me, Savannah. He needs a good woman in his life. I grew up with him. I know Cruz, and I'm one of the very few women in this world who can look at him objectively. He's drop-dead gorgeous, but he's lonely."

Lonely? Right. The man couldn't make a move

without stepping on a woman who was throwing herself at him. "The two don't go together."

"Yes, they do," Vanessa insisted. "Sure, he's been with a lot of women and they all flock to him, but he's right in what he thinks."

"What do you mean?"

"It's the cowboy they want to be with. The handsome wrangler who gives them something to fantasize about when they go back to their pricey worlds and their polished crystal stemware and their socially acceptable suitors with spreading waistlines. Cruz knows this, and he hasn't let anyone close to him." Vanessa smiled affectionately at her. "Until you."

Afraid she would begin to believe her, Savannah started to turn away.

Vanessa caught her by the shoulders, holding her fast. "I can see it in his eyes when he looks at you," she insisted. "You don't want him for a fantasy, and he has no idea what to make of you or what to do with you."

Savannah thought of the night she had just spent. "Oh, I think he has some idea what to do with me."

Vanessa laughed just as Devin peered in through the front door. Vanessa help up her forefinger. "In a second," she called out. Looking at Savannah, she hurriedly continued. "I think that the best thing that could happen to him is if you married him."

Savannah knew Vanessa meant well, but this wasn't helping the situation. There were only three words she needed to be convinced to marry him, and they wouldn't be coming from Vanessa. "You're my best friend. You have to say that."

"No, I don't," Vanessa said firmly. "And I never say anything I don't mean. My point is that Cruz needs someone like you in his life. I'll go one step further. He needs *you*. And I think you need him."

Vanessa was right. She did need him, but that too was something she wasn't about to share. Not until she was convinced that he wanted her—and not just a clear conscience.

"What I need right now," Savannah announced, "is a shower. And you need to go to Devin before he takes root over there, waiting for you." She gestured toward the entrance.

Vanessa glanced toward her husband. "All right, all right, I'll go. But that doesn't mean I'm giving up on this." And then she hugged Savannah tightly. "Stop thinking of everyone else for a change, and just think of you."

Savannah only smiled in response as Vanessa released her. She *was* thinking of herself. She was remembering herself as a little girl. A little girl with an enormous burden on her shoulders. She didn't want that happening twice in her life. More than anything, she didn't want to ruin two more people's lives the way she had ruined her mother and father's.

Though they spoke on the telephone almost daily, the house seemed incredibly empty to Savannah without Vanessa there. Ryan had assured Savannah that she was welcome to remain at the house for as long as she wanted to. He urged her to think of the Double Crown as her home now. With the furniture from her former apartment now housed within the two spacious rooms that comprised her private living quarters, the Double Crown could very well have become her home.

But a feeling of restlessness wouldn't leave her. Savannah felt as if she was in transition, as if she hadn't found her real place yet. She figured it was probably due to the pregnancy. She hadn't gained any weight yet, but because her stomach had finally settled down, she was no longer losing it either.

Without Vanessa to share her thoughts with, Savannah found herself spending more time with Cruz's sister Maggie and her five-year-old son, Travis. She adored all children, and Travis was no exception. Sensing a kindred spirit, the boy gravitated to her, and she enjoyed playing with him and reading to him when Maggie was through house-keeping for the day.

"You're really great with kids, you know? All he can talk about is you."

Savannah grinned as Travis ran to her, crying out, "Sa-hanna!" She figured it was close enough. In her arms, Travis snuggled against her. He smelled of the outdoors and cookies. "He's learning to be a real ladies' man, like his uncle."

"His uncle could take a few pointers from him," Maggie said, sitting down on the front steps of her parents' house. Maggie looked at her. "You know, you could have a real gentling effect on him."

"Travis is great just as he is."

"I was talking about Cruz."

Savannah laughed as the boy made himself at home on her lap, presenting her with a picture book.

"I really doubt any woman could have a gentling effect on Cruz. Besides, I wouldn't want to change him. He's perfect just the way he is."

"Perfect?" Maggie hooted. "Please, if you have an ounce of compassion in you, don't ever let Cruz hear you say that. His head is big enough as it is." She rolled her eyes. "Perfect, ha!"

"But he is." Knowing it was what Travis

wanted, she began to slowly bounce him on her knee. The little boy started giggling and clapping his hands. "He's sensitive and exciting, and after you get used to how good looking he is, he's easy to talk to."

"See, that's what I mean." She gestured to underscore her point. "You talk to him. Most women aren't interested in what he has between his ears—not that there's much," Maggie tacked on with a mischievous smile. "They're more interest in what he has between the pockets of his tight jeans." She bit back a laugh at the surprised look on Savannah's face. "What they don't think of him as is a person. But you do."

Above Travis's protest, Maggie shifted him from Savannah's lap to the floor. "Play with your toy now, honey. Savannah and I have to talk."

"Sounds ominous," Savannah commented.

Maggie moved closer to Savannah, lowering her voice so they wouldn't be overheard. "Why *did* you turn Cruz down when he asked you to marry him?"

"Because he asked me out of a sense of duty and honor."

Maggie looked puzzled. "From what I hear, those are very good traits."

They would be, if they were in addition to the

all-important one: Love. "For a boy scout, maybe. I'm not a merit badge."

Savannah debated saying anything further. But Maggie had befriended her, and she seemed genuinely interested in her happiness. So Savannah tried to make her understand her position. "If a man asks to marry me, I want to know it's because he loves me. Because he can't face a day without me. Not because his sister or his conscience tell him it's the right thing." She saw Maggie begin to protest, and cut her off. "I want his heart to tell him it's the right thing."

"And if his heart did all this talking," Maggie hypothesized, "then you'd say yes?"

It was on the tip of Savannah's tongue to say yes, but she couldn't. There was more in the way than just that. "Maybe."

Maggie's brows drew together. "Only maybe?"

Savannah rose and began to pace. "There's another problem. Cruz wants a horse ranch of his own." She knew she wasn't saying anything that Maggie didn't know. He'd probably shared this with his family long before he had done so with her. "He wants it more than he can breathe." She turned and looked pointedly at Maggie. "If he has to think about supporting the baby and me, he can't put every dime he makes into his dream, now can he?"

"And once this baby is born, you're planning on becoming a hermit?"

Travis took the opportunity to grab hold of Savannah's arm and tug urgently. Without missing a beat, she stooped down and scooped him up into her arms. "What?"

"Staying close to home, doing nothing except care for the baby," Maggie elaborated. "Not working for the Fortunes anymore."

The idea of not working was absurd. She loved pulling her own weight. She always had. "No, of course not. I'll take off a few weeks, then keep the baby with me as I work."

Maggie spoke slowly, as if she was trying to digest every syllable. "You're talking about your immediate plans, aren't you?"

"Yes." That was exactly what she was planning to do: have the baby, then return to work as soon as she was physically able. Rosita had already come to her and insisted that she be the one to watch the baby while Savannah worked.

"So why can't you do that if you're married? Why can't you go on working as if you were a single mom, even if you're married? You can provide for yourself and the baby, and Cruz can continue saving for his dream ranch."

It sounded perfect, but nothing ever was. Savannah shook her head. "You're oversimplifying it."

"No, I'm not," Maggie insisted. "Think about it."

There was no need to think about it. "It's a moot point. Your brother asked me once, and I turned him down. He used up his supply of male pride. He's not about to ask me again." Suddenly, she could see exactly what Maggie was thinking. "And don't you make him."

Maggie only laughed at the idea. "Maybe you don't know him as well as I thought. Otherwise, you'd know that no one can make Cruz do anything he doesn't want to do." She rose to her feet and took Travis from Savannah. "Bedtime, little man."

Travis began to whimper in protest. He turned soulful eyes toward his protector, but Maggie turned him away so that Savannah wasn't subjected to the pitiful ploy.

She shushed her son's protest. "Men, they're all alike. Always trying to resist what's best for them." She looked at Savannah just before she crossed to the threshold. "All I ask is that you promise to think about what I said."

Savannah knew she could spend from now until doomsday thinking about it. It wouldn't change anything. The moves, the words, all belonged to Cruz.

But to placate Maggie, she murmured, "I promise," and hoped that would be the end of it.

Twelve

Savannah frowned as she looked at her reflection in the mirror. Putting aside the dress she'd been holding up against her, she stood sideways and looked again.

There was no doubt about it. She was starting to show.

After all these months, her waist was beginning to thicken just a little. It wasn't really enough to make anyone notice, unless they were looking closely for telltale signs.

But *she* had been. Every day for the last five months—ever since she'd discovered that she was pregnant—Savannah had examined herself in the mirror each time she dressed. Waiting to see the signs that her body was nurturing another life within it.

Now the signs, long overdue, were here, and she wasn't sure just how she felt about it. About anyone else seeing her body widening with life. Mixed emotions churned through her. Savannah pressed her clasped hands to her lips.

It was finally happening.

There should be no mixed emotions, she thought sadly. It should be a happy time. It *was* a happy time—but only when she thought of the baby, not the circumstances.

But her circumstances refused to hang back in the recesses of her mind for very long. She was a single mother. She could give the baby love, but not a father. At least, not beyond the biological sense of the word.

Damn, Savannah thought, reaching for her dress, when were these hormones of hers finally going to settle down and stop creating all these tears? Ever since she'd become pregnant, it was as if her emotions had gotten thrown onto a train repeatedly running up hills, only to plummet down the other sides.

This couldn't go on. She had to get hold of herself. She had a baby to think about. And a future to create for both of them.

Giving herself a pep talk, Savannah slipped the deep-green velvet dress on and let the wide, soft skirt glide over her body. With a high neck and long, straight sleeves, the dress was festive and flattering. No one looking at her could guess that she was pregnant, much less six months along.

Slipping on her heels, she took a deep breath and went out to join the others.

Downstairs, the house was subtly decorated to reflect the Thanksgiving holiday. Floral arrangements of rust, deep gold and orange were tastefully set out in the foyer and adjacent areas.

People were already filling the house, and the sound of voices blending in simultaneous conversations rose to greet her before she reached the bottom step. Ryan was having his traditional Thanksgiving dinner, attended only by family and those who worked on the ranch. There'd be another larger dinner tomorrow night, where friends would be invited.

Trying not to be too obvious, Savannah looked around to see if Cruz was here. Maggie had warned her that Cruz might not come. It usually depended on his mood as to whether he would make an appearance.

Savannah didn't see him—

She blocked out the pang that followed on the heels of the realization that he wasn't here. It really wasn't a surprise. Of late, she'd only seen him in passing. It was as if that night in his cabin hadn't even taken place. Days would go by, and she wouldn't catch so much as a glimpse of him at all. Someone told her that Cruz had taken to working with the horse in the meadow. She wondered if he was purposely avoiding her, shutting her out.

She could easily have ridden out to where he

was, using some pretext or another. But that's what it would have been—a pretext. And he would have seen through it. A woman had to draw the line somewhere, and she had already drawn hers when she'd turned him down.

But her common sense had turned him down, not her heart.

It was better this way, she told herself firmly as she smiled and returned greetings that came her way. She'd given Cruz her answer—now it was up to her to stick by it. The time for regrets was long gone.

"Hey, look at you," Dallas enthused, coming up behind her. He enveloped Savannah in a warm hug. Gone this last month, he had arrived home in time for Thanksgiving. "Motherhood agrees with you, Savannah. You're positively glowing."

She pretended to fan herself as he released her. "I think it's just the heat."

Dallas laughed.

He'd had no intention of attending the dinner. For one thing, though he bore no ill will to Ryan personally, to Cruz the whole idea seemed patronizing: "Senor" Fortune throwing his doors and his table open to "the help" and having them mingle with his own family.

But that wasn't his only reason for skipping the

meal. For days he'd been avoiding seeing Savannah. She'd turned his proposal down, even after they'd made love again. Not verbally this time, but the message was still unmistakable. A man's pride could only tolerate so much, and seeing her would be like rubbing salt into the wound created by her rejection. So he kept his distance, figuring that eventually this would all be a memory.

Cruz had no idea how many days made up an "eventually," but he had a feeling the number was a lot higher than he anticipated.

But his decision to forgo Thanksgiving was not without repercussions. His father's displeasure, though never dark, never censuring, was still not something he relished facing. The fact that he was a grown man and on his own made little difference.

Ruben Perez had sent his wife, daughter and grandson along to the main house while he stopped at his son's cabin. He knew that Cruz, without being prodded, would not be attending the party. He intended to prod.

"You're not ready."

The shrug that met his father's statement was purposely casual. "I'm not going."

"Yes, you are."

Cruz met his father's eyes unflinchingly. "I'm too old to bully, Dad. I can do as I please. And I don't want to attend Ryan Fortune's Thanksgiving dinner.''

Ruben shook his head as he frowned. Instead of anger, there was disappointment in his eyes. Cruz would have preferred anger. "I never thought I'd live to see the day my son was a coward.''

Cruz's eyes darkened at the affront. "I'm not a coward.''

Ruben looked mystified that there could be any doubt. "You're running from a small, blond woman. What would you call it?''

Cruz blew out a breath, curbing his temper. He couldn't allow himself to shout at his father. "I'm not running. I proposed, she turned me down.'' And that was the end of it. "I can't drag her off by her hair and make her marry me.''

"No,'' Ruben readily agreed. "But you can face her.'' He knew his son, understood his heart even when it remained such a mystery to Cruz. Life had taught him things. "No matter what you try to tell yourself to the contrary, that's why you're not going—because you'll have to see her there. If your conscience was clear, you could face her.''

Cruz was losing his hold on his temper. Struggling to maintain control, he waved a hand at his father. "You don't know what you're talking about.''

"Fine.'' Ruben inclined his head amiably. "I

don't know what I'm talking about." He moved in front of Cruz as his son tried to turn away. "Prove me wrong. Attend the dinner."

He knew what pride meant to his father. And his absence would be noticed by Ryan. Cruz weighed sides. "Does it mean that much to you?"

"Yes," Ruben replied quietly. "It means that much to me."

Surrender seemed inevitable. He'd gone head to head with his father before, and even when he won, he felt as if he lost. There seemed no point in this confrontation. A quick grin of affection flashed across his handsome face.

"All right, I'll go."

A softer, subtler smile graced Ruben's features. There was a candle burning in the church he attended regularly. It represented a silent prayer that the parents of his grandchild would find their way into each other's lives. But being a down to earth, sensible man, Ruben knew that God helped those who helped themselves and he was more than willing to be on God's team.

"Good." Sitting down, Ruben made himself comfortable on the worn leather sofa. "I'll wait while you change and get ready."

"Yes, I'm sure you will." With a resigned laugh, Cruz went to get dressed.

* * *

He walked in just as Savannah was being embraced by Dallas. The sudden flare of emotion he felt cut through all the lies he'd been telling himself. He hadn't put her from his mind. On the contrary, she was more entrenched there than ever.

And Cruz had absolutely no idea what he was going to do about it.

It was as if she had radar. Savannah knew the instant Cruz walked into the house, even though there were people between them, blocking the way. She'd already told herself not to expect him, and thought she could deal with his absence calmly. But his presence was another matter. She felt her heart stop, then start again, pounding as if she'd just run a record-breaking mile.

Like an orchestrated scene in a movie, their eyes met across the foyer. Suddenly, it felt as if sunshine had slipped into her body, despite the gray skies outside.

She barely heard Ryan above the roar in her ears.

"Well, now that everyone's here," Ryan announced jovially, looking at Ruben, "I believe dinner can finally be served."

It took her a moment to realize that Dallas was presenting his arm to her. "If you'll do me the honor, I'd like to escort you to the dining room, milady," he teased.

She saw Cruz stop abruptly, but there was nothing she could do. She couldn't very well tell Dallas that she was waiting, hoping that Cruz was coming toward her.

And then an idea came to her from nowhere, like lightning across the clear sky. "Of course—if you promise to let me bend your ear a little. I have a proposition for you."

"Sounds promising."

Cruz heard Dallas's deep laugh and something in his gut tightened in angry response.

As she walked into the dining room with Dallas, she quickly outlined her idea.

He looked at her thoughtfully, then smiled. Clearly Savannah and her idea had taken him by surprise. "I'll give it some thought," he promised.

"That's all I ask." Mentally, she crossed her fingers.

Dallas helped her with her chair, then glanced down at the place card next to Savannah's setting. He shook his head as he smiled. "Looks like we won't be sitting together. I'll discuss this with you later."

Before she had a chance to read the name on the setting beside hers, she saw Dallas exchange a few words with Cruz. The next moment, Cruz crossed to her and sat down next to her.

Feeling oddly flustered, her eyes met Vanessa's

across the table. The other woman winked. The seating arrangement suddenly made sense: Vanessa had been in charge.

"If you'd rather sit somewhere else..." Savannah began quietly. She didn't want him next to her if it made him uncomfortable.

He wondered if she was politely telling him to go elsewhere. Would she have preferred Dallas next to her? Cruz tried to shake himself free of the wave of jealousy that was becoming annoyingly familiar. "This is fine."

With voices buzzing around them, she and Cruz began their meal in silence.

He could sweep any woman he chose to off her feet with absolutely no effort, he thought, yet he felt tongue-tied and awkward sitting beside Savannah, searching for a way to begin a conversation. Each made conversation with the people sitting on their other side, but not with one another.

It struck Cruz as ironic: she was the only one he *wanted* to talk to.

Glancing toward her, he noticed that the small portion of food she'd taken had hardly been touched. Was she feeling ill? "You're not eating."

His voice, low and gentle, startled her. She offered a quick smile, a fleeting movement of her lips, nothing more. "I nibbled while we were preparing it."

Ryan had toasted Lily for the meal and his mother for all the meals that graced the Fortunes' table the other 364 days. Cruz raised a brow. "You cooked this?"

"Some of it." She down-played her part, though she'd enjoyed helping. "Lily couldn't have managed preparing the entire meal alone."

Cruz took a sip of his wine, watching her. She looked nervous, he thought. Was it because of him? Some of his own unease faded. "I just thought Ryan was paying lip service when he toasted Lily for preparing the meal. I thought this was really catered."

"No, it was made right here in the kitchen." As she spoke, she became more animated. "Ryan wanted to have it catered, but Lily insisted on making it a home-cooked meal. Vanessa and I volunteered to help her and Hannah."

"Hannah, but not Maria?" He asked after Lily's other daughter.

Lily had pretended it didn't bother her, but Savannah knew it upset the woman a great deal to have Maria refuse to help.

"From what Vanessa tells me, Maria's behavior is becoming more and more erratic." It had been, so she'd been told, ever since Bryan's christening. "Lily asked her to at least attend dinner, but she refused that, too. Maria gave her some excuse about having to be somewhere else." It hadn't even been an elaborate lie. Savannah shook her head. "If I had a mother who cared that much about me, I would certainly shown up."

If. The word echoed in his head. How could your own parents not care about you? Inclining his head, he lowered his voice. "Is that why you're here instead of home for Thanksgiving?"

She refused to read concern into his question, refused to allow her feelings to soften toward him any more than they already were. "This is my home, at least temporarily."

"What about your parents?"

Out of habit, her voice became distant. Savannah had made up her mind a long time ago that the only way to excise the hurt from her life was to keep everything that had to do with her childhood and her parents under wraps.

"We don't speak much. I send cards on their birthdays and the holidays, but..." Her voice trailed off and she shrugged.

His eyes were kind. "What about them—do they send you cards?"

No, it wasn't going to hurt, it wasn't. She had enough to deal with in the present without going back to the past for more.

Savannah pressed her lips together, toying with the dark circle of cranberry jelly on her plate. "My parents are busy leading separate lives.'' Raising her head, she looked at Cruz, defying him to offer her pity. ''They got divorced as soon as I went off to college. Sold the house, picked up the threads of lives they'd abandoned eighteen years earlier.'' *Shutting me out.* ''So you see,'' she concluded with forced brightness, lowering her eyes again, ''there is no 'home' for me to go to. They've each started lives that have nothing to do with me whatsoever.''

Cruz couldn't understand people like that—people who could emotionally abandon their own flesh and blood. He was grateful for the family he had, even though at times he wanted them to butt out of his life.

''Their loss,'' he told her quietly.

She raised her eyes to his. This time, the smile began in her eyes. ''Thank you.''

He hadn't said it to be thanked. He'd said it because it was true. Uncomfortable with her gratitude, he indicated his plate. The healthy serving he'd helped himself to was all but gone.

''This is very good. You really should eat some.'' His eyes skimmed toward her belly, his meaning clear.

She picked up her fork. ''All right, I'll eat for one.''

''One?''

"I'm not hungry," she explained quickly. "But maybe the baby is."

Relieved there wasn't something seriously wrong that she wasn't telling him, he smiled at her. "Maggie said Travis was born hungry."

Her eyes strayed toward the boy who was sitting between his mother and grandmother. With his combed-down hair and pint-size suit, he was apparently on his best behavior tonight. She hardly recognized him. "That's because he's made out of pure energy."

The warm look in her eyes did not go unnoticed by Cruz. "Maggie tells me you're very good with him." He was summarizing a long speech his sister had delivered on more than one occasion, singing Savannah's praises and filling his ear with things that she'd done with Travis, like starting to teach him to read despite how young he was. "She thinks you'll make a good mother."

Savannah hoped the words were prophetic. "I know I'm going to try. I love children, I always have. Having one of my own will be like holding a miracle in my arms."

Even as she said it, she couldn't quite believe it. She was going to be a mother. To have a child of her own. Part of her still wasn't convinced, despite the ritual of looking at her waist in the mirror and her bouts of morning sickness, that she was actually going to have a baby.

He looked at her. "Yes, I can see how it would feel like that."

The conversation grew easier, and they spoke as the dinner drew on.

A half hour later, Savannah pushed back her plate with a sigh. "I shouldn't have had that much." Once she had gotten started eating, it had been amazingly simple to continue. Now she felt utterly stuffed.

Standing behind her, Cruz helped Savannah with her chair. "I'm sure the baby appreciates the sacrifice you made. Maybe a little fresh air'll help." Taking her hand easily in his, Cruz began to lead her to the terrace. But he stopped as they passed Lily. "The meal was delicious, Mrs. Redgrove."

Lily beamed at the compliment. "Thank you, Cruz. I know I don't hold a candle to your mother, but it was certainly fun trying."

She sounded sincere, and he appreciated the tribute she gave his mother. Maybe he'd been too quick to judge everyone so harshly. Maybe he'd do better to be a little more easygoing before labeling those around him, he decided.

The air on the terrace was chilly, quickly erasing any sluggishness that was beginning to take hold because of the large meal. Taking a deep, bracing breath, Cruz glanced toward Savannah. He saw her shiver.

He took off his jacket and slipped it around her shoulders. His hands lingered as he drew the front of the jacket together. Cruz looked down into her face, emotions stirring. "I've missed you."

She couldn't have kept the smile from her lips if she had tried. The simple words warmed her far more than his jacket did.

Now that he had told her, she didn't want him feeling guilty about it. "You've been busy. How's the horse coming along? Quicksilver, right?"

He laughed. "Quicksilver reminds me a little of you. Small, proud and stubborn. Lucky for me, she can be bribed with a lump of sugar."

"So that's your secret with women. Sugar. And here I thought it was your devastating charm."

One eyebrow rose higher than the other. "Devastating, huh? Doesn't seem to have worked on you."

Her hands were partially hidden beneath his jacket, and she pressed them now against her belly. It was like touching a secret. Except it really wasn't a secret anymore. "I think it worked all too well on me."

It amazed him how quickly desire flared in his veins. One minute, it was all under control; the next, it was taking him prisoner and promising no mercy.

"Prove it."

Without a word, Savannah turned her face up to his, the invitation clear. It was more than he could resist. Desire broke through the final restraint. All the needs he'd been trying to lock away, to unsuccessfully ignore, came to life, rattling cage doors that hadn't been shut firmly enough.

He'd tried very hard not to think about her. Friday nights would find him going to town with his friends, trying to lose himself amid the anesthesia of inconsequential encounters. Without fail, women would seek him out, asking him to buy them a drink, interested in a night of passion with no strings attached.

He found himself ignoring them the way he wanted to ignore her. The only trouble was, he couldn't ignore her.

Unable to deny himself, his mouth found hers, and it was as if he'd found his way home again. Cruz took her into his arms before he could think better of it. And then, there was no room to think at all.

Thirteen

Cruz really hadn't wanted to come to the party in the main house. But once he'd allowed his father to talk him into it, he'd silently vowed that if he saw Savannah, nothing was going to happen between them. He wouldn't let himself be alone with her, wouldn't let himself kiss her, and above all, he wouldn't let himself bring her back to his cabin where either of the above could have dangerous consequences.

From where he stood right now, it looked as if he wasn't going to be able to keep a single promise.

Cruz wasn't completely sure just when the decision to return to his cabin had been made, or by whom. Had he suggested it, or had she? Or did it just evolve?

All he knew was that kissing Savannah on the terrace robbed him of his sanity, his ability to remain detached.

Just as it always did.

A man shouldn't want a woman who messed up

his mind, whose very existence threatened to up-
heave everything in his life, uprooting foundations
along the way and making him lose sight of the
simplest of things. Like which end was up.

A man shouldn't want a woman like that.

But *he* did.

He no longer had any answers. All Cruz knew
was the length of time that had gone by since
they'd last made love, down to the second. All he
knew was that if he couldn't have her tonight, he
wouldn't live to see the light of dawn.

"Come with me," he whispered against Savannah's mouth. The entreaty was pressed between
two soul-igniting kisses.

How the word "no" turned into "anywhere"
was completely beyond Savannah. She heard it at
the same time Cruz did. And knew her fate was
sealed. But then, she'd had her suspicions about
her fate almost from the start.

They slipped away quickly, leaving the party be-
hind. Cruz took her to the stable where he'd left
Hellfire. He didn't bother saddling another horse.
Every second was precious.

The sky they rode beneath was beautiful and
dusted with stars now, a sharp contrast to their last
night together.

"I saw this once in a western," Savannah told
him after he'd set her on his horse and mounted

behind her. His body pressed tantalizingly close to hers as they rode. "And thought it was hopelessly romantic."

"And?"

She turned as far as she could in the saddle, her face inches from his. Her heart raced just to look at him. "I still do."

Unable to wait, Cruz bent his head, his lips capturing hers in a quick kiss. He tasted strawberries and a smile.

Savannah's eyes shone with humor in the moonlight. "At this rate, we'll get to your cabin by Christmas."

Cruz kicked his heels into the stallion's flanks, urging the horse on more quickly. "I can't wait that long."

A wildness surged through Savannah's veins, as she gloried in his confession.

The night was everything she expected.

And more.

Like two kettles heated to the limit and about to boil over, their passions spilled out on one another the moment they were inside the door.

With lips hungrily feasting and hands questing over one another, they shed each other's clothing, sending it all flying. Garments fell, slipping into shadows—along with the rest of the world.

The only thing that existed was the fire that blazed between them. All that mattered was quenching it.

But it refused to be quenched, or even managed.

The more Cruz kissed her, the more Savannah returned his ardor, the higher the flames rose.

Desire ravaging him, Cruz drew his head back, suddenly aware of how rough he was being. Concerned, he paused. "I'm not hurting you, am I?"

"Only if you stop," she breathed.

Framing his face with her hands, Savannah brought his mouth back to hers. And paradise back to her life.

They made love wildly, as if they had never touched before. As if they both knew that when morning came, with its intrusive light, all this would be forever over, nothing more than a dream to be secretly treasured.

They had tonight.

He raked his hands over her body, so warm, so giving, astounded that within this fragile, soft vessel, a child of his was growing. It seemed impossible.

He felt his heart swell, and gave up telling himself that it was the moment, the mood, the madness that was seizing him. It was more, much more.

Cruz had been a passionate lover from the first, but this went beyond anything she'd experienced before in his arms. Savannah struggled just to draw air into her lungs. He seemed determined to pull it all away from her, to leave her gasping, fulfilled and praying for more with her last dying breath.

She arched against him as she felt his mouth on hers again, wrapping her legs around his hips and urging him in. Urging him to take her before she had no strength left to complete the journey with him.

It was a night that would forever be burned into her soul.

Consciousness crept over him in small, fuzzy layers, each a little brighter than the last. And with consciousness came contentment. He smiled before his eyes were opened. Smiled and reached for her.

His hand touched air. The sheets were cool.

Awake now, he looked at the place beside him in the bed where he had last enjoyed her. It was empty.

He didn't have to get up and look through his rooms to know she wasn't in the kitchen, or anywhere else in the cabin. She was gone.

Cruz curbed the impulse to drag on his clothes and go looking for her. Maybe she needed time. Maybe they both did. He fell back in bed, folded his hands beneath his head, and stared up at the beams in the ceiling. Thinking.

Last night had been a revelation as to the extent of his feelings. He and Savannah had made love several times, each a little slower than the last, a little more tender than the last. And finally he'd realized that no matter how many times he made love with Savannah, he was never going to get his fill of her.

That was the greatest realization of all—that he would always continue wanting her. It shook him down to the core of his being, but Cruz was determined to come to terms with this and find a place for it in his life.

He'd never thought he'd ever care for just one woman.

He'd never thought he'd care at all.

So for now, he gave her her space. And sought his own.

Anxious, excited, Savannah rapped softly on Dallas's door, then listened for some sound of movement on the other side. It took everything she had not to just go bursting in the moment she arrived back at the house. But she wanted Dallas to give her a positive answer on her proposition from last night. And being woken up at a fairly early hour the day after Thanksgiving by a wide-eyed madwoman wasn't conducive to the kind of answer she was hoping for.

She'd been unable to sleep after Cruz had drifted off at her side. The hours had ticked away as her brain feverishly made plans. Wonderful plans. Plans for Cruz—because with all her heart, she wanted him to be happy. And if he was happy, maybe then there would be a place for her in his life.

Eventually, she couldn't remain lying still any longer. So she'd gotten dressed and quietly slipped out of the cabin, taking care not to wake him.

Because they'd ridden his horse there, she had had to borrow Hellfire to get back. But she hadn't left Cruz stranded. There was an old Jeep parked behind the cabin that he occasionally used to get around when he wanted to spare his horse, or when he was going into town. She had a feeling that he didn't exactly like lending out his horse, but she couldn't wait until he was awake. She wanted to find out if Dallas had an answer.

The *right* answer.

"C'mon in, the door's open."

When she slowly turned the knob and ventured into the huge suite, she found that Dallas was already up and dressed. Good, she wouldn't have to talk to a half-sleeping man, apologizing for barging in while she tried to convince him to agree to her plan.

Dallas grinned when he saw Savannah. He gestured over to the plush cream-colored leather sofa against one wall. "I had a hunch I'd be seeing you. Have a seat and let's talk."

Savannah crossed her fingers.

Patience was something Cruz had never completely gotten the hang of. Even though he could exercise it when he was training a horse, when it came to people, the same talent eluded him.

Standing in the small corral, he looked up at the main house. He had work to do, but he couldn't keep his mind on it. He'd found his horse in the stable. Why she'd ridden back alone instead of waking him up to take her back was beyond him.

He tried not to think about the possible reasons.

Though he attempted to block it, he had this overwhelming desire just to see her. He'd give her space if that was what she wanted. He wouldn't crowd her about marrying him. Maybe for the time being, it was even better this way.

But he wanted to see her. Just *see* her, nothing more. She was like a fever of the blood, and the only cure seemed to be further exposure.

He gave up pretending he could get any work done this morning. Taking the lariat from about the horse's neck, he murmured, "Wait here," then swung over the railing to the other side.

He ignored the curious looks of the other wranglers in the immediate area and headed toward the back entrance of the main house. Coming in through the unlocked door, he went to Savannah's office first. "Why did you leave so quickly—"

The question was posed to an empty room.

Curious, and a little worried because he knew how dedicated she was to her work, he headed upstairs to her room. Was she sick? he wondered. Had he been too rough with her, after all?

Biting off a curse at his own thoughtlessness, Cruz took the stairs two at a time, hurrying up the wide staircase. He reached the landing in time to see Savannah coming out into the hall.

Out of Dallas's room.

Cruz froze, watching. She looked radiant.

Backing out of the room, Savannah hardly knew what to say to express her gratitude. They were friends, but that didn't mean Dallas owed her anything. "I can't begin to tell you how very grateful I am."

Dallas laughed. "I'm the one who should be thanking you for this unexpected opportunity." He touched her face. "Tell Cruz he's a very lucky man."

As if anyone could tell Cruz anything. "I don't think he'd feel—" She stopped abruptly, feeling someone else's presence in the hall. And then she saw him, saw the dark anger in his face. Was something wrong? "Cruz, what are you doing here—?"

His throat had tightened so hard that he could barely speak. The taste of bile was in his mouth.

"Apparently finding out just how big a jackass I am." Turning on his heel, Cruz raced down the staircase—before he gave in to the overwhelming urge to punch Dallas's face in.

How could he have been such a colossal idiot? Savannah had slipped out of his bed only to go to Dallas's.

Savannah couldn't begin to guess what he was thinking, only that she had to set it right before it got out of hand. Without a word to Dallas, she flew after Cruz.

"Cruz, wait, where are you going?" But he didn't even turn around. "Cruz, talk to me," she demanded.

He'd never known he could feel such rage— such hurt. It was as if someone had ripped open his chest and yanked out his heart while it was still beating.

"Go talk to your lover," he snapped. "Don't waste your time with me."

"Lover?" The accusation stunned her into immobility. "Are you out of your mind?"

He stopped on the stairs to look at her over his

shoulder. The contempt in his eyes nearly made her stumble backwards.

"I was, but not anymore." Turning away, he felt her hand on his shoulder, trying to stop him. Without thinking, wanting only to get out of this house, he shrugged her off—

The scream he heard froze him in his tracks. Everything happened so fast, the images only registering afterward: Savannah, tumbling past him, falling down the rest of the stairs. Dallas, yelling behind him. His own heart pounding so hard that he was sure it was cracking in two.

Cruz plunged after her, managing to catch her arm just as she reached the bottom. But she'd hit her head in the fall and was unconscious. Like a doll made of cotton batting, she lay limply in his arms when he gathered her to him.

For the first time in his life, Cruz didn't know what to do. Tears filled his throat.

"Oh, my God, Savannah. Savannah I didn't—" His voice cracked. Fighting panic's grip, Cruz touched her throat. There was a pulse. He looked up as Dallas reached them. "Call an ambulance." Cruz felt her stirring. *Oh, God, please let her be all right.* The prayer thundered through his brain.

"No," Savannah said weakly, "it's all right. I just had the wind knocked out of me. I'm—" The rest of the sentence was cut off as she sucked in air through her teeth, wincing. And then her eyes fluttered shut as she slipped back into unconsciousness.

It was then that Cruz saw the smear of blood on the stairs.

Lifting her in his arms as gently as he could, Cruz rose to his feet. There was going to be no debate. He wasn't about to take any chances. She needed a doctor, and she needed one now.

"The hell with the ambulance. I'm taking her to the hospital myself."

Dallas was already ahead of him, opening the front door. "I'll drive. You stay in the back with her."

The fight had been drained out of him. Cruz made no protest. All that mattered now was Savannah.

Dallas watched Cruz pace around the small waiting area. He looked like a panther moments away from leaping out of his skin, Dallas thought.

They hadn't exchanged two words since the emergency room doctor and nurses had taken Savannah away. Cruz had to be threatened with expulsion before he finally retreated from the examining room, letting the ER physician treat Savannah without him.

Dallas tried to remember when he'd ever seen

Cruz so concerned, so upset. He drew a blank. His sympathies went out to the other man.

"She'll be all right, Cruz."

Cruz didn't bother looking at Dallas. He'd turned his anger inward. "It's my fault if she's not."

Dallas came up behind him. He couldn't stand idly by and watch Cruz beat himself up over what happened. "It was an accident."

That didn't make it any less his fault, Cruz thought. He looked at Dallas. "One that could have been avoided if I wasn't stupid enough to think that she'd eventually settle for someone like me." There was resignation rather than accusation in Cruz's eyes as he regarded Dallas. "Not when you're around."

It took Dallas a second to process what Cruz had just said. When he did, it still didn't make any sense. "What the hell are you talking about?"

Cruz laughed shortly. Did Dallas think he was blind? "Don't pretend, Dallas. I saw her coming out of your room."

"So?" He stared at Cruz. What the hell was he getting at? "Pretend what?" And then, with the force of a collapsing ten story building, it hit him. Dallas's eyes widened at the sheer stupidity of the accusation. "You *are* a jackass, you know that?"

"Yeah, for thinking that—"

Angry, Dallas cut him off. "For thinking that I would try to take someone from you, or that she's the kind of woman who would go after someone for what she could get." They'd played together, grown up together. Cruz should have known better. More than that, he should have known Savannah better. "If Savannah were here right now, I know I wouldn't have to defend her. I'd have to hold her back from tearing you apart." Dallas struggled to control his temper. "She didn't come to my bed, you blind idiot. She came to my room."

Cruz's eyes became dark slits. "The difference being?"

He was going to have to spell the whole thing out for him, wasn't he? Dallas didn't know if Cruz had suddenly become too stupid, or too much in love to think clearly. For Savannah's sake, Dallas sincerely hoped it was the latter.

"The difference being that she came to talk about you."

"Me?" Cruz stared at him, dumbfounded. "Why?"

Dallas knew that Savannah would have wanted to tell Cruz himself, but he couldn't stand by and let Cruz think that she'd betrayed him like this.

"She asked me to invest in your dream." And that was another bone he had to pick with Cruz. What had happened to their friendship over the years? "Hell, Cruz, if you wanted to start a horse ranch, why didn't you tell me? I would have been more than happy to—"

"To what? Give me money?" He wasn't about to accept charity from Dallas, or anyone else. "I didn't want to ask you for money."

"So you'd rather ask a bank?" Cruz had no collateral, only his abilities to trade on. Banks didn't make loans based on things that weren't tangible. Dallas knew what a beating his pride must have taken to even go to a bank. "We go back a long way, Cruz. You owe me the privilege of sharing in your happiness. I'd hate to lose you, but I can't think of anyone who could make a better go of a horse ranch than you."

All the anger that Cruz had harbored, dissolved like soap bubbles carried on the wind. "That's what she was doing in your room? Talking about the horse ranch I want to build?"

"That's what she was doing in my room. Trying to make what you wanted a reality. She's a hell of a woman, Cruz. And you owe her a hell of an apology."

He owed her much more than that, Cruz thought. And it might take the rest of his life to make it up to her. Cruz sank down on the sofa and dropped his head into his hands. "God, I've been such a jerk."

Dallas sat down beside him. He laid a hand on Cruz's shoulder in silent camaraderie. "Glad we can agree on something."

Savannah reemerged out of her haze slowly. Every inch of her ached and tried to pull her back into the numbing mist. Struggling, she resisted, trying to remain above it.

The first thought that came after the pain had stabilized pierced her heart. She remembered tumbling, the stairs rushing up at her. Hitting her head—

The baby. Was the baby all right?

Frantic, Savannah rooted around for the buzzer. Finding it, she pressed down hard, ringing for the nurse. Her mind ticked off the seconds, waiting.

No one came.

She couldn't lay here not knowing. She had no idea whether she was still pregnant or not. Gripping the side of the bed, she pulled herself up into a sitting position. She had to find someone to ask.

The room swayed as she tried to get out of bed. It whirled even faster when she closed her eyes. The headache pressed down on her, threatening to knock her out.

Savannah gripped the side railings tightly, trying to steel herself so she could swing her legs over the side of the bed.

"Hey, what do you think you're doing?" Coming in response to the call, the redheaded nurse hurried into the hospital suite. She reached Savannah's side in time to push her gently back into bed. It didn't take much effort.

Savannah felt light-headed, breathless. She struggled to hold onto consciousness. "I wanted to find someone—my baby—is my baby…?"

Gentle, capable hands were tucking her into bed. "You're baby's fine. But you won't be if you go waltzing around the hospital at this hour."

"This hour?" Savannah repeated dumbly. The last she remembered, it was just before nine in the morning. "What time is it?"

The disembodied voice emerged from the haze. "It's almost midnight." Someone was smoothing the blanket around her. "Now try to get some rest. The doctor wants you to stay overnight to make sure that you're all right. If you don't behave, I'll make him keep you here longer."

Longer. No, she didn't want to stay longer. She wanted to see Cruz. To explain.

Realizing her eyes were shut, she fought to open them again. A woman was leaning over her. Red hair. The nurse. Savannah tried to wet her lips.

"You're…absolutely sure the baby's…all right?"

"I'm absolutely sure. Want something to help you sleep?"

Savannah could feel herself sinking, shrinking away. "No," she whispered.

She didn't have enough strength to move her lips and ask the nurse about Cruz. But her last thought was of him....

Fourteen

"Is she all right?"

Cruz pulled the towel he'd been using to dry his hair away from his face and rested it on his damp, bare shoulders. He'd returned home less than half an hour ago to grab a quick shower. His body ached. The past night had been spent sitting in a hospital chair designed for discomfort.

Dallas had finally gone home early in the afternoon, but Cruz had been afraid to leave—afraid that if he did, Savannah or the baby would take a turn for the worse. It didn't matter that a doctor had assured him that both were unharmed and doing fine. He'd wanted to make sure himself. The only way he could do so was to keep vigil through the night.

Ruben's expression was anxious as he looked at his son, waiting for an answer. Word had spread through the ranch about Savannah's accident.

"She's fine, Dad. The doctor said she could leave the hospital sometime this afternoon." And he intended to be the one to take her home, no matter how hard she might protest. He had a lot to make up for.

Ruben nodded. "And the baby?"

The grin flashed quickly. Savannah and the baby had been lucky. They'd all been lucky. Especially him. "Fine, too."

Ruben made the sign of the cross. "How about you? How are you doing?"

"Me?"

It was on the tip of Cruz's tongue to question why his father felt he had to ask how he was faring, but then he decided there was no point in continuing the charade. Ruben had seen through him from the first. He usually did. As he grew older, Cruz realized that his father was a great deal smarter than he had ever given the older man credit for.

Cruz rubbed the remaining moisture from his hair. "I'm doing okay."

But Ruben had his own take on that as he studied his only son. "You're doing nothing."

Cruz had already begun walking back into the bedroom. He had to get dressed and going if he wanted to be sure that he was the one taking Savannah home. "What?"

Ruben followed his son into the bedroom. "You want to know what I think?"

Cruz opened a drawer and took out fresh underwear, then found a new shirt in his closet. "I'm sure you'll tell me whether I ask or not."

Ruben's eyes narrowed. "Don't get smart. I think you're afraid to love this girl."

The truth hit closer than he was comfortable with. Dropping the towel, Cruz quickly got dressed. "Careful, Dad."

Ruben's frown deepened. "There's such a thing as being too careful. You have all these ideas about women and love, but you are afraid to risk loving this particular woman. Afraid to give your heart because you think it might be rejected. And—"

Cruz interrupted him. "There is no 'think' about it, remember? She's already said no to my marriage proposal."

Ruben continued as if Cruz had said absolutely nothing. "That ranch you are so committed to having—it's just an excuse, something to help protect you from making what you think is a big mistake. You know what's the biggest mistake of all?" He handed his son his boots as Cruz pulled a pair of socks on. "Turning your back on love. *Not* risking your heart. If you don't risk, you don't win. Me, I have your mother, your sisters, you. I am the winner here. Would I be more of a winner if I had a big ranch and no one to share it with me? Don't trouble your head—I can give you the answer to that. No.

"Now go back to her and tell her what is in your heart." He tapped his son's chest with his index finger. "She will listen."

His father was preaching to the choir, but because the man had gotten up such a large head of steam, Cruz let him say his piece. Then he played devil's advocate. "She didn't listen before."

Ruben shook his head. "That's because you didn't tell her before." He looked pointedly at Cruz. "Tell her now. Open up your heart to her and let her see for herself."

It was a scary proposition, but his father was right. If he didn't risk, he wouldn't win. And he wanted to win.

Cruz didn't even bother holding back the smile. "Maybe I will."

Peering into Savannah's room, the young nurse looked around. Seeing only Savannah, she seemed a little disappointed. "Did he come in?"

Savannah looked at the nurse blankly. "Did who come in?"

There had been a procession of visitors to see her this morning. Dallas had stayed for a little while, as had Vanessa, Claudia and Matthew, and Ryan along with Lily. Vanessa had insisted on paying all the hospital bills, using the excuse that Savannah worked for the Double Crown Ranch.

Backed up by her father, Vanessa had refused to take no for an answer, so Savannah gave up trying, silently grateful and vowing to pay Vanessa back the first chance she had.

Savannah pushed aside the swivel table with her lunch tray. The doctor had told her early this morning that if everything continued as it had, he'd discharge her at three. Though she wasn't really hungry, she knew she needed her strength. Besides, she had a feeling that the blustery physician was not above having her tray checked to see if she was eating. She was taking no chances; she wanted to get home. Get on with her life. She needed to put a few things in perspective.

The look on the young nurse's face indicated that as far as she was concerned, there could be no mistaking who she was referring to.

"That good-looking cowboy." A hint of a sigh escaped her lips as she adjusted the blood pressure cuff around Savannah's arm and took a reading. "The other nurses told me he spent the night stretched out on a chair in the hallway." Her eyes sparkled, and for a second she lost the thread of what she was doing. "Long, straight hair the color of midnight. Warm eyes like a puppy's." Aware that she'd drifted, she glanced at the numbers and noted them before deflating the cuff. "Someone tried to get him to go home and come back later, but he said he wasn't leaving until he was sure you were all right.''

Finished, she returned the gray cuff to its place and took Savannah's pulse—which jumped just as she touched it. A knowing smile slipped over the nurse's lips.

Cruz. No one else fit that description, Savannah thought. So he *had* come to the hospital. But if he'd been here, why hadn't he come into her room?

The nurse had to be mistaken. Cruz wouldn't have spent the night in the hall. He didn't care enough to put himself out like that.

Savannah shook her head. ''No, he's not in here. He hasn't even been to see me.''

Incredulous, the nurse took out a thermometer attached to a gauge and slipped a plastic covering over it before inserting it under Savannah's tongue. She kept her eyes on the gauge.

''Men, go figure 'em. I know I can't.'' She withdrew the thermometer and threw out the see-through covering before she wrote down the reading.

Savannah sighed, laying back against her pillows. ''You're not alone.''

The nurse was about to make another observation when the door behind her opened. She turned around in time to see Cruz walking in.

Her wide mouth split into an even wider grin of satisfaction. Her eyes darted toward Savannah. "Speak of the devil." Cheerfully, she made a last notation, then closed the clipboard and picked up the tray from the table. "I'll just leave the two of you alone."

She winked at Savannah as she backed out the door.

Puzzled, Cruz shoved his hands into his pockets. He'd thought of bringing flowers, but knew that such an offering couldn't begin to convey the things he wanted Savannah to know. He'd bide his time. The way he figured it, if he was lucky, he'd have the rest of their lives together to give her flowers. All kinds of flowers.

He nodded toward the closed door. "What was that all about?"

"She was just sharing a philosophy with me." His face was drawn, she thought. The look in his eyes when he saw her yesterday outside Dallas's room came back to her. Savannah took a deep breath. She had to get this misunderstanding cleared up. "Listen, Cruz, I have to explain."

But he waved away her words. "You don't have to explain anything."

He was telling her that he didn't care enough to waste time listening. Determination galvanized her. "But I want to."

A fresh wave of guilt washed over him. He wasn't accustomed to feeling guilty, and he hated it. "Dallas told me what you were doing in his room."

Maybe she should just let it drop right here, but suddenly, she felt a sharp stab of pain that any of this had even been necessary. Savannah raised her chin. "He shouldn't have to tell you anything. You should have known you could trust me."

Cruz shrugged, feeling oddly helpless. Just as helpless as he had when he had gathered her, unconscious and bleeding, in his arms. He could only offer her the truth. "Trusting women isn't something that comes easy to me."

It was a blanket statement, and she didn't like being herded in with other women who had meant nothing to him. After all she'd been through, she'd made up her mind to mean something to him.

"Sorry to hear that. Does that apply to your mother and sisters?"

The question irritated him. "You know that's different."

"No, apparently I don't know anything." Like what her place was with him. She didn't want to be at arm's length and if that was the way it was going to be, then maybe she had better rethink everything—and put some distance between them as soon as she was able.

Primly, she smoothed out the blanket that lay across her hips. "Well, if you talked to Dallas, then you know you can go ahead with those plans for your ranch now." Dallas had promised her to have everything in place for the loan by Monday. "It's what you need—"

Cruz laughed shortly at the choice of words, not knowing whether to be amused or annoyed. "You, too?"

She looked at him sharply. "Me, too, what?"

"Everyone keeps telling me what I need." And he'd just about had his fill of all these well-meaning Samaritans. Cruz's voice rose as he spoke. "My father tells me what I need. My mother tells me what I need." He thought of Maggie's talk with him over a month ago. No wonder it had taken him this long to pull his thoughts together. Who could think with everyone coming at him like B-52 bombers? "My sister tells me what I need. *You* tell me what I need." He found himself standing right beside her. "What I need is for everyone to stop telling me what I need."

Hurt, but determined not to show it, Savannah drew herself up. "Did you come here to yell at me?"

"No!" He was going about this all wrong. Cruz blew out a breath. Women rarely said yes when they were being shouted at. With effort, he lowered his voice. "No, I came here to tell you what I *really* need."

"Oh?" She couldn't help being leery, even though part of her felt the prick of anticipation.

He took her hands in his, feeling unnaturally awkward. How the hell did someone propose? Maybe just this once, he should have asked his father for pointers. "I need you."

Stunned, her lips formed a perfectly round circle. "Oh."

A warmth spread inside him. Maybe he hadn't made a complete mess of it, after all. "Yes, 'oh.' I want you to marry me."

Because she wanted it so badly, she refused to believe that Cruz meant the proposal the way she wanted him to. That was hoping for too much. And any less was unacceptable.

She tried to draw her hands from his. "Look, if this is some kind of payback in gratitude for Dallas's backing your ranch—"

His hands tightened around hers, refusing to release her. Damn it, when would she get it through her head that wanting her was not tied to his having a horse ranch?

"Dallas and I agreed to an interest rate. Nobody said anything about handouts."

The comment would have made her laugh if her heart hadn't been so sorely involved. "All right, then if it's because you feel responsible for the baby—"

"I *am* responsible for the baby," Cruz pointed out. "At least in part. Half the genes in that baby are mine."

Suddenly weary, she closed her eyes. "Fine, nobody's disputing that. But you don't have to marry me. I already told you that."

How many times, she thought, did he want her to say no to something she desperately wanted to say yes to? But she wasn't her mother. She couldn't wield guilt like a scalpel, cutting into his sense of decency and leaving a wound that would never heal.

It was all or nothing. She couldn't allow herself to accept anything short of that.

Exasperation colored his voice. "Can't you get it through your thick head that I know I don't *have* to marry you, that I *want* to marry you?" What did he have to do to make her understand? To make her agree?

For one brief, heady moment, the very breath was temporarily stolen from her. But when she found it again, Savannah managed to ask, "Why?"

He looked into her eyes. "Because I love you," he said softly.

Her heart leaped, but she banked down the surge of emotion. He was still doing "the right thing."

He must have been talking to Maggie, who had probably told him what Savannah had been holding out to hear.

"Just like that?"

"Yes—and no," he admitted. The only road to follow was the honest one—and hope for the best. "Maybe I started loving you the first time I saw you, I'm not sure. I've reacted to a lot of women over the years. Strongly to some." But that was all physical passion, and there was so much more at play here.

"I thought you were no different." He lifted her hands to his lips and pressed a kiss to each. "But you were. I kept thinking about you. Even before you came back to the ranch, I was thinking of heading on up to Dallas on business and maybe looking you up." Cruz abruptly stopped himself. "No, no more half truths," he said with determination. She would be won with honesty, or not at all. "I was going to look you up. The business trip was just an excuse."

Savannah's jaw slackened just a tad. This was far more than she'd ever hoped for. This time, there was no way she could rein in her hopes.

"You were really going to look me up?"

"Yes." If he was going to tell her the truth, he had to tell her all of it. "Because I wanted to prove to myself that you didn't have the sweetest lips,

"Put your money where your mouth is," Savannah challenged.

"I'd rather put my mouth where your mouth is." Sitting down again, he gathered her to him.

Savannah began to laughed. "Cruz, you wouldn't—"

But he would.

And they did.

Epilogue

"Just a little further. You're doing great."

Savannah felt Cruz's hand at her elbow, guiding her. Her eyes covered with a silk bandanna, she kept her hands stretched out before her, anticipating contact. But all she felt was air. They'd left the confines of the Jeep where he'd originally covered her eyes before beginning this journey, and, from what she could gather, they were still outdoors. But where?

"Is there something about you I should know, Cruz? You're not into anything kinky, are you?" She asked the question teasingly. "I mean, blindfolds, long winding car rides, mysterious behavior. Just what have I gotten myself into?"

"An endless supply of love, for openers." His excitement had gone from a Kentucky two-step at the outset of this trip to a frantic jitterbug at its final destination. What if she was disappointed? Cruz tried not to think about that. Instead, he concentrated on positioning her in exactly the right place. He wanted her first view to be breathtaking.

His face close to hers, his fingers on the ends of the bandanna, he asked, "Ready?"

Excitement swirled through her. What was all this about? She could feel the wind whistling softly around her as it passed rough fingers of winter along her face. "I was ready ten seconds after you put the blindfold on me—hours ago."

He laughed. "You have no concept of time. It wasn't hours ago." He didn't have to glance at his watch to know how long it took to get here. He knew the route by heart. He had clocked it and traveled it a great many times since he'd made his decision. "Twenty minutes to be exact." With a flourish as pregnant as the woman he'd recently made his wife, Cruz undid the knot and pulled the bandanna away. He held his breath as he gestured around. "Well, what do you think?"

She blinked once, and then again, before staring, stunned by what was before her. Nature had laid itself out beneath her feet as neatly as a painted scene on a calendar. "I think you tied the blindfold too tight. I'm seeing things."

"What is it you think you see?"

The valley below, even swaddled in autumn colors, was lush and vibrant. "The most beautiful view I've ever laid eyes on." She turned toward Cruz, an unspoken question in her eyes. "It's gorgeous."

He let go of the breath that had stopped up his lungs. "It's yours. Ours," he amended, almost tripping over his tongue in relief and happiness. Taking Savannah's hand in his, he spread his other hand out wide. "This is where the ranch house will be." Every syllable was bursting with pride. He loved this land. Almost as much as he loved her. "I wanted to show it to you as soon as I had the deed in my pocket." His eyes held hers. "So you wouldn't regret marrying me."

How could he even think that? "I don't regret marrying you, and it had nothing to do with what you have in your pockets." She was just going to have to convince him, she thought. The prospect was not without its appeal. "I didn't marry you for what you could give me materially, Cruz. I married you because of what you did to my heart—" mischief curved her mouth "—and because you're a hell of a kisser."

He laughed, taking her into his arms. But he was serious in his intent. He never wanted her to regret becoming his wife. "No, really." Cruz pressed a kiss to her forehead. God, but he loved this woman. "I know the wedding left a little something to be desired." It had been a hurried affair, thrown together in the space of six days that were mostly a blur.

Her smile reached up and touched him. "No, it didn't."

He raised a dubious brow. "Yeah, right. Every woman dreams of being married in her best friend's living room with just a few people present—most of them her new in-laws."

Savannah pretended to sniff indignantly. "I don't know about most women, but it suited me just fine. And don't you go saying anything against my in-laws. I like them a lot." Raising her left hand, she angled it so that the gold band caught the sun and gleamed. "Besides, this is what counts." Her eyes shifted to Cruz. "This, and you."

He covered her hand with his own. There was a matching band on the third finger. "You're a rare woman, Savannah Clark."

She raised her chin. "That's Savannah Clark Perez—and don't you forget it."

His arms closed around her. "I don't intend to. Ever."

They were going to be happy here, she thought. Very happy. And very lucky. "Show me where the bedroom is going to be."

Releasing her, Cruz looked around. He took her hand, walked a few feet, then paced off a length. Finished, he announced, "Right here."

"I like it." Tilting her head, she raised her mouth to his invitingly.

Having no reason to resist, Cruz drew her to him. The kiss he brushed against her lips deepened until it pulled them both in. Savannah felt her body heating as he slipped his hands beneath her jacket. A purr of contentment echoed through her as she felt his fingers exploring. "What are you doing?"

The grin made his mouth look sultry. "Just breaking the room in."

"Ah."

Cruz kissed the grin from her face. And felt it enter his soul—where it remained.

* * * * *

Here's a preview of next month's

***Super-wealthy widower Dallas Fortune
wrangles for a bride and an heir in
A WILLING WIFE
by
Jackie Merritt***

Maggie Perez couldn't think of one sensible thing to say to Dallas Fortune. *Why are you here?* was just too blunt, although that particular question was definitely at the root of her confusion. Unnerved, she slammed the door shut a little too hard.

Dallas grinned. Obviously he was ruffling her feathers, which was a good sign that he was right about her preferring a man to *be* a man.

His smile broadened. "How are you today?"

"Fine," she said stiffly. "I'm fine. And you?"

"Right as rain," he quipped.

Maggie was beginning to remember her manners. "Would...would you like something cool to drink? There's fresh lemonade in the refrigerator."

"Thanks, I'd love a glass of lemonade."

Grateful that she had dusted and vacuumed the house that morning, Maggie said, "Go on into the living room. I'll get the lemonade."

"Thanks." Dallas went one way, Maggie another.

When she walked into the living room a few

minutes later with two glasses of lemonade, Dallas was standing at the one window in the room from which he could see Travis playing in the yard.

Dallas accepted a glass and said, "That's some boy you have, Maggie. You must be very proud of him."

"Yes, I am." She sat on the sofa. "Sit anywhere," she told him.

"Thanks." Dallas chose her father's favorite chair and took a big swallow of his lemonade. "This is good. Getting back to Travis, I asked him how old he is and he said, 'Ten.'"

Maggie nearly choked on *her* lemonade. "He said he was ten? He's five!"

Dallas laughed. "He also said, 'I'm tough.'"

Maggie groaned. "He wants to be tough so badly, and I don't think he even knows the true meaning of the word."

"He's all boy, Maggie. Let me ask you something. Would you mind if I took him riding sometime?"

"He's never been on a horse, Dallas. Papa told him he would teach him to ride, but he hasn't had the time yet."

"I'd put him on our most gentle horse, Maggie, and guarantee his safety. For that matter, you could come with us and see for yourself that he's all right."

While she was thinking of an answer to that request—which troubled her—or *trying* to think of an answer, Dallas's expression became caressing and intimate. "Know what I'd like to do right now?" he said softly. "Make love to you, Maggie. You're just about the only thing I've thought of since we talked yesterday."

She knew she should feel insulted—no man had ever spoken his mind so clearly to her before—and she was almost stupefied because she felt overheated and achy in personal places.

"You...you don't mean what you just said," she whispered hoarsely. "We don't even know each other."

"We grew up together."

"Knowing each other as kids doesn't mean we know each other now."

"You're evading the issue. Will you go out with me tonight?"

Maggie felt as though a steel band around her chest was getting close to cutting off her air supply. "So we...we can make love? How dare you even suggest such a thing?"

"You're trying very hard to be angry, aren't you? Surely you don't prefer that a man hide his true feelings and seduce you when you're not looking." Dallas set his glass on the table next to his chair and then leaned forward. "Maggie, with you

I think everything should be out in the open. I was struck dumb by you yesterday. You're one of the most beautiful women I've ever seen, but there's more to you than an incredible face and body. You hit me precisely where it counts for a man, and I thank you with all my heart for that.''

"So I should sleep with you just because you...you feel grateful for something I didn't even know I did?''

"Not sleep, Maggie. I doubt that we'd be doing much sleeping. I need to know something. Where's your husband?''

"You don't even know I'm divorced, and you're asking me to go to bed with you? That does it!'' Jumping to her feet, Maggie angrily advanced on the crudest man she'd ever known. "So you want to take Travis riding? You louse, you actually have the gall to use my son as an excuse to get to me! Well, read my lips, *Mr*. Fortune. I will never, let me repeat, *never*, have one personal moment with you! Is that clear enough?''

She'd made a tactical error. Dallas recognized it, Maggie didn't. In her fury she'd gotten close enough to Dallas that it was a simple matter for him to reach out, take her by the waist and pull her down on his lap. She didn't want to scream and risk scaring Travis outside, but she wiggled and fought and did her best to scratch out Dallas Fortune's whiskey-colored eyes!

"So you're a little wildcat," Dallas said with a satisfied laugh after catching her flailing hands in his. "I figured you were. Come closer, little wildcat, and let me tame you."

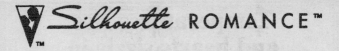

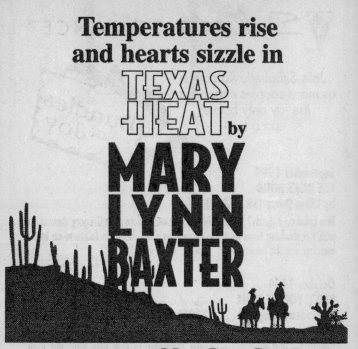

Membership in this family has its privileges...
and its price.
But what a fortune can't buy,
a true-bred Texas love is sure to bring!

If you missed any of *The Fortunes of Texas* series,
act now to order today!

The Fortunes of Texas

#65030	**MILLION DOLLAR MARRIAGE** by Maggie Shayne	$4.50 U.S.☐ $4.99 CAN.☐
#65031	**THE BABY PURSUIT** by Laurie Paige	$4.50 U.S.☐ $4.99 CAN.☐

(limited quantities available)

TOTAL AMOUNT	$
POSTAGE & HANDLING	$
($1.00 for one book, 50¢ for each additional)	
APPLICABLE TAXES*	$ _____
<u>**TOTAL PAYABLE**</u>	$ _____
(check or money order—please do not send cash)	

To order, complete this form and send it, along with a check or money order for the total
above, payable to Silhouette Books, to: **In the U.S.:** 3010 Walden Avenue, P.O. Box 9077,
Buffalo, NY 14269-9077; **In Canada:** P.O. Box 636, Fort Erie, Ontario L2A 5X3.

Name: _____

Address: _____ City: _____

State/Prov.: _____ Zip/Postal Code: _____

Account # (if applicable): _____ 075 CSAS

*New York residents remit applicable sales taxes.
Canadian residents remit applicable GST and provincial taxes.

Silhouette®

EXTRA! EXTRA!

The book all your favorite authors are raving about is finally here!

The 1999 Harlequin and Silhouette coupon book.

Each page is alive with savings that can't be beat!

Getting this incredible coupon book is as easy as 1, 2, 3.

1. During the months of November and December 1999 buy any 2 Harlequin or Silhouette books.

2. Send us your name, address and 2 proofs of purchase (cash receipt) to the address below.

3. Harlequin will send you a coupon book worth $10.00 off future purchases of Harlequin or Silhouette books in 2000.

Send us 3 cash register receipts as proofs of purchase and we will send you 2 coupon books worth a total saving of $20.00 (limit of 2 coupon books per customer).

Saving money has never been this easy.

Please allow 4-6 weeks for delivery. Offer expires December 31, 1999.

I accept your offer! Please send me (a) coupon booklet(s):

Name: _____

Address: _____ City: _____

State/Prov.: _____ Zip/Postal Code: _____

Send your name and address, along with your cash register receipts as proofs of purchase, to:

In the U.S.: Harlequin Books, P.O. Box 9057, Buffalo, N.Y. 14269

In Canada: Harlequin Books, P.O. Box 622, Fort Erie, Ontario L2A 5X3

Order your books and accept this coupon offer through our web site
http://www.romance.net
Valid in U.S. and Canada only.

PHQ4994R